Contents

WAITING ON YOU

WAITING ON YOU

SARA BELLCAMP

1

Chapter 1 - Meet Cute

*B*randon Fyfe.

    I stared at the name on the gold star plastered to the door of the huge deluxe trailer (basically, an uptown loft on wheels) and I couldn't help the sullen look on my face.

You chose this life, I reminded myself all over again. *This is the life you chose.*

Shuffling the clipboards in my arms in the dim light, I sidestepped a puddle on the ground to give way to several grips walking by carrying boom mics and equipment across the lot toward the only warehouse that was still bustling this late in the day.

Stage 31.

The fluorescent lights flickered and blinked on the light posts up and down the way, as if they too were already exhausted from being on all the time.

It wasn't an entirely new feeling.

Exhaustion had been on the job description at my last work too.

Even though spending over a year as a temp, doing all sorts of jobs at all hours, all across the Tri-State Area, wasn't the distinguished life my family would have deemed acceptable. Not after working so hard with the just-as-sleepless nights in college, working on papers and projects to complete an illustrious degree in Computer Science.

Really, it was Princeton's fault for offering one of the best computer *and* humanities programs in the country. So while I was working on my major, in what my friends would have called my 'typical overachieving fashion', I'd managed to take some units alongside to complete a degree in Film Studies as well.

But some things in life, you just couldn't help.

My first love had always been film.

Not the glitz and glamor of the limelight though.

Always fascinated by the process of creating movies, my dream was to be involved with everything that went on behind the scenes. To learn the magic, the ins and outs of what it took to produce Hollywood blockbusters. To get a privileged peek at the everyday workings of the biggest names in the industry, perhaps to be able to pick the brains of the best directors in the world. Like Spielberg or Lucas.

Something about that cliché line "You are the sum of the five people you spend the most time with."

So instead of making use of my computer degree, much to my parents' chagrin, I'd passed up a chance at that lucrative career and spent the last year and a half trying to network. To grow my connections to break into the movie business.

Though I still liked to think I was diligent and level-headed.

A very few things truly excited me.

Finding out I'd gotten the job as a Personal Assistant to one of the legends in the business, the tough-as-nails producer of *Lightscape* Studios, Debra Winger? In Hollywood?

I had totally screamed. I was ecstatic for days.

The connections I would gain from this position alone? They would certainly only open even more doors for me.

Not that I was a mere dreamy-eyed fresh grad with dreams of Hollywood. I'd already cut my teeth, so to speak to a degree, working a few short but stressful stints at some off-Broadway theaters. I was looking forward to digging further into the nitty-gritty of production life. I wasn't looking for shortcuts. I was very much aware everyone needed to start at the bottom.

The tiny apartment I shared with my friend Annie in the heart of LA, the only thing I could afford, was definitely a testament to that.

But—I never imagined bottom would look like this.

Or if this wasn't the bottom, it surely looked a hell of a lot like it.

Sighing, I cast a glance at the haggard caterers refreshing the tables, setting up for the long night ahead. I was already well aware from familiarizing myself with Debra's calendar that the current production was three months delayed. I was one week into the job as Debra's PA Lauren's assistant when

I was asked (more like volun*told*) to sub as a PA for (AKA babysit) the most delinquent actor in the production.

Brandon Fyfe.

Of course, I already knew who he was. I'd seen some of his movies, some of his TV shows. I'd read his entire bio on Wikipedia.

Born in Boston. Only son to his parents Bob and Lisa—a dentist and an art director. Discovered at the age of fourteen. He was a teen idol before he moved on to more mature roles. His paranormal TV series 'Love Bites' propelled him to worldwide fame where he played Connell Rhodes, an often heartbroken vigilante monster hunter.

Although the Wikipedia article never mentioned that Fyfe's second personal assistant *of the month* had unexpectedly quit on him for undisclosed reasons.

Not a good sign.

I fidgeted on my feet as I waited. I almost felt like I was being given the chance to run away, get a head start on escaping the potentially horrible situation. But I steeled myself. The toughest players in Hollywood would no doubt have even more difficult demands or crazier personalities and I would need to adapt and rise to the occasion.

Debra's voice inside the trailer got louder and I snapped to attention. Craning my neck, I strained to make out the conversation through the small gap in the door.

"Fyfe, for crying out loud—"

"Fine! Fine." The deep, smooth voice of the person Debra was talking to was already tinged with exasperation. "Let's pretend I even have a choice in the matter, shall we? Bring on the next challenger poser wannabe ambitious twerp. Honestly Deb, do you even take the time to vet these people or do you just pull them off the street?"

"This may come as a surprise to you but my main function is not actually to constantly search for someone to put up with your crap. I'm only letting you borrow this one until the end of production and you'd better make this work or the next time, you're going to have to fetch all your imported coffee beans straight from Nicaragua yourself."

He let out a snort.

"Oh, by the way," Debra paused. "She's pretty."

Overhearing that, my eyebrows snapped together in puzzlement. What was that supposed to mean?

A sentiment echoed by the amused voice from inside the trailer. "What's that supposed to mean?"

"Fyfe, I'm going to ask you again for the last time. Your last three PAs were all anywhere between blonde or even remotely attractive, and in the end, for whatever reason, they all up and quit within two weeks—"

There was a chuckle of someone sounding highly pleased with himself. "I still maintain none of that was my fault—"

"Did you or did you not sleep with them?"

I chewed on my bottom lip.

Needless to say, Brandon Fyfe was also well known for his disarming smile and intensely magnetic on-screen charisma. And in his sixteen-year acting career, he'd allegedly had fourteen girlfriends, a possible average of one per year. Or at least these were the ones the studio had allowed to make public.

The response was a bemused scoff. "I swear to god, Deb. I didn't. I know better than anyone you won't stand for that crap, and I have way too much respect for you." He paused. "Besides, I'm pretty sure you have ties to the mob and I really didn't want to be disappeared," Fyfe's next statement bore no remorse whatsoever, as if he didn't even care he was being reprimanded.

At least, I was well aware that Debra Winger had a zero-tolerance policy on misogyny or harassment of any kind in her company. It was one of the reasons the job offer had been so appealing, but still...this was definitely not a good sign.

Some shuffling made me look up as Debra swung the door open fully. Impatiently shaking her short graying hair out of her eyes, she waved her hand. "Come in."

I made an effort to straighten up my face from a cringe as I stepped up and into the trailer to meet my new charge. I swallowed hard before looking up, instantly meeting his blue eyes.

Brandon Fyfe.

His bio said he was six-foot-two inches but he looked taller. His sandy blond hair was just a touch shaggy. His eyes looked significantly darker blue than in his headshots, but it was likely caused by the dim light in the trailer. He was wearing a designer shirt, black slacks, and a hint of make-up, as though he'd just come from a publicity event.

He met my gaze and openly gave me a critical once-over.

I gave his obvious once-over a look of disbelief.

"Brandon, this is Rye Williams."

I did a small nod. "Nice to meet you." I cast a glance around the trailer. It wasn't slob central but I could see Fyfe had started a pretty massive collection of coffee canisters on the floor in the corner. There was a stack of scripts on the table and several trophies lining the window. I spotted a couple of People's choice awards among them. There were no family pictures or personal effects. The TV mounted on the wall was on mute and showing reruns of 'Bewitched.'

"Hmm... She is pretty," Brandon remarked. But then he added, "Looks kind of uptight though."

His comment caught me off-guard. My jaw dropped. "Um...I'm standing right here," I pointed out, unable to help a stunned glance up to Debra to check I hadn't just imagined it.

Debra pursed her lips. She was obviously used to his antics. "Brandon, be nice. Don't make me take away your 'walkies' privileges like last time. Be a grown-up for once, please." Her focus went to the mobile phone in her hand. "We've got about six weeks to get this all wrapped up before I start severing heads and I'd really hate to make everyone work through Christmas again. Rye, you got family?"

Her question was snapped at me, I jumped. "Um, no. I mean, yes. I mean, whatever you need, Miss Winger."

Brandon shook his head in mirthful disbelief.

"Good," Debra replied curtly. "I don't like hearing 'family emergency' excuses. I'm not saying it's not okay. I'm just saying your job better be done before you tell me you have to leave early because your ex-husband can't pick up your kid from school or that you're taking two days off to bus to Vegas to attend your parents' fiftieth wedding anniversary. I'm trying to run a business here."

Brandon's eyes lit up. "Oh, was that Simon's parent's fiftieth? Now that's impressive." He whistled.

Debra's steely gaze narrowed on him for a moment before she turned to me again. "Make sure he's at make-up by six tomorrow. I've asked Lauren to send you all his information, his schedule, riders, stuff he needs. It should be in your e-mail. Read it tonight. And if you have any questions, ask Lauren." She gave me an even look that carried a potential hint of a semblance of reassurance. "Look, I know this is un-expected, but that's the job, do you understand?"

I nodded again. "Of course, Miss Winger. I understand."

"Good." Debra beckoned me over so we could leave. "Fyfe, don't make me rewrite your contract again. You're lucky I cut you slack because the ratings are hanging in there."

"Wouldn't dream of it." He moved to see us off.

Debra shot him another dark glare as she and I exited the trailer and headed away.

"Either way, Debra, you've got nothing to worry about," Brandon yelled out after us. He leaned against the door-frame, his arms across his chest, his tone fully teasing. "And if there ever was anything exciting, I'll be sure to leave a spe-cial sock on the door for you, and rest assured, you'd be more than welcome to join."

I made a face in revulsion and even more disbelief even as I quickened my pace to get away as fast as possible.

Ladies and gentlemen, Brandon Fyfe.

2

Chapter 2 - Day One

I had been knocking on the trailer door for over fifteen minutes. "Mr. Fyfe. They need you at make-up." Turning to lean beside the door, I muttered to myself, "I mean they needed you at make-up a half-hour ago, but whatever."

The studio was already busy with streams of staff walking purposefully back and forth across the lot despite the early hour. Then again, I was aware that sometimes they did shoots throughout the night.

I rubbed my eyes. I figured the previous night was probably the last one that I would be getting as much as six hours of sleep for the next six weeks.

Though I'd also spent quite a few hours reading through Lauren's files to familiarize myself with Brandon Fyfe's information. I'd always been a quick study and I wanted to stay ahead of the game if I was going to impress Debra. Not that my new client's information didn't make for entertaining reading.

The guy had a list of requirements probably longer than Beyonce's.

I'd read that Van Halen's tour rider once demanded M&M's with absolutely no brown ones. I figured it was as crazy as performer mandates went.

Fyfe's was close.

No sweets. No carbs. No beer. And mints. Dear god, he had to have mints everywhere. Sugar-free, of course.

Lauren's file also included quite a long list of Fyfe's "offenses," not the least of which was that he tended to show up late to shoots for whatever reason. That one in particular was likely going to be a challenging thing to deal with.

I checked my watch for the time, not even bothering to turn around as I rapped harder on the door. "Mr. Fyfe? Hello? You're super late now."

After another two minutes of shifting on my feet, I let out an exasperated groan. "Oh, for god's sake." I pulled out the spare keys from my pocket to unlock the door myself and opened it with a swing.

"Mr. Fyfe?" I stepped up into the trailer but it was clear the moment I laid eyes on the enclosed space that my client wasn't inside.

Cursing under my breath, I walked past the kitchenette and the leather couch before charging toward the room in the back. I even checked inside the toilet.

He was definitely not in there.

"Oh, you gotta be kidding me." I hurried out the door again. I blew out a breath, my hands on my hips as I looked around, at a loss.

"Brandon gone again?"

I whirled around. I squinted to recognize one of the make-up artists from across the way.

The slight, lanky guy, wearing a gray silk vest with suede boots was standing by the door to the studio offices. He was probably also on the lookout for Fyfe.

"Uh, yeah." I raised my hand to gesture. "It's Vic, right?"

"Victor, if you like. Hi." With a smile, he came closer to offer his hand to shake mine. "You're new, huh? Welcome to the third act of the most delayed production ever."

I broke a smirk. "Um, thanks?"

Victor waved his hand. "Not that it's all Brandon's fault. We also had problems with budget cuts and drama with the higher-ups. Honestly, it hasn't been Debra's lucky year."

I shrugged. "Well, so far I'm only in charge of this one problem. I'm so sorry to be holding you all up."

"I'm sorry to say we're all used to it." Victor grinned. "Lauren gave you the list though, right?"

My eye lit up at the recollection and I pulled up my phone to find another particular list from the Brandon Fyfe files.

Apparently, Brandon had well-known "escapes"—places he was known to hide in, holes in the wall. I supposed it was now up to me to check out each haunt until I found him. Like a scavenger hunt. I scrolled through the list, already making a face. "What is this? The Irish Pub, Shiatsus on Seventh, L4 gym on Bleecker, Cece McEntire—is that a clothing store?"

Victor gave me a pointed look.

I rolled my eyes. "Right." If I had to bust in on him while he was with some bimbo groupie, there was no timer fast enough to track how fast I would quit this job. I groaned out loud right as my phone rang. I glanced down to read the Caller ID.

Lauren.

Uh-oh.

Victor craned his neck to have a nosy at my phone himself. "Better get started, sweetie," he advised. "The clock is ticking."

This was nothing, I told myself as I raced around the city to hunt down my client.

One time last year, I had to make two hundred sandwiches at a hospice charity event, at the same time that I had to tutor an upstart twelve-year-old, and then deliver a truckload of balloons across town whilst battling Manhattan rush hour traffic.

I shook my head briskly to clear it and refocus.

This was nothing, I tried to convince myself yet again.

Taking the steps up to the fourth floor of an austere sort of building two at a time, I huffed as I spoke into the Bluetooth headset attached to my ear. "Yes, I think I've finally found him."

The production coordinator had been calling Lauren every fifteen minutes in the past couple of hours, and then Lauren had been calling me.

Brandon Fyfe was keeping a staff of about sixty waiting, sitting around, burning a hole through Debra's bottom line.

I glanced up at the sign on the wall and turned left following the arrow labeled "Dr. Blumenthal." I should have known one of the places on his list was a shrink. I clenched my jaw. This was absolutely not how I saw my first day on the job going.

I plowed through the door, despite the notice "Ongoing Session."

"Oh, hey, my limo is here." Brandon was reclined back on a La-Z-Boy armchair, his long legs stretched out across the area rug as he nonchalantly announced my presence. "Dr. Blumenthal, this is my new PA, Rye Williams."

I stood at the open doorway as I stared at him. "Do you have any regard for anyone but yourself?"

"Doc?" Brandon simply turned toward his shrink, the late-forties female psychiatrist, sitting behind her desk across from him.

"No, not really," Dr. Blumenthal responded for him. "Mr. Fyfe suffers from the typical narcissistic and entitled behavior common for his type of employment, possibly stemming from his career peaking way too early, but we are still exploring other underlying factors."

I shot her a flat look then looked back over at my charge with a dark glare. "I've just been to three bars, two spas, and had to creatively misdirect a very fanatical woman in the Arts district looking for you. This was my eighth stop."

"And it only took you two hours. Congratulations," Brandon drawled.

I gave him a suffering look. "Everyone is waiting for you, your highness. Lauren has been calling me nonstop all morning. You're going to get your pampered butt off that couch and into the car downstairs."

Brandon chuckled as though he was used to empty threats.

"NOW."

My tone somehow made Brandon turn to glare up at me. "Or what?"

I tilted my head at his obstinacy. "Whatever it is, I imagine I'd be breaking my NDA, but I assure you, I'd be more than happy to."

A bemused smirk on her face, Dr. Blumenthal leaned back in her seat. "I see you've built a rapport with this one."

I snapped to attention. My expression instantly neutralized to give the doctor an apologetic please-don't-shoot-the-messenger sheepish look. "It's my first day."

Dr. Blumenthal's eyebrows shot up in surprise. "It is? Interesting." She turned to Brandon slowly, looking exceedingly curious.

Brandon rolled his eyes. "Oh my god, okay." Pulling a lever with a crank, he pushed up off the chair. "I'm not paying you to speculate about irrelevant things."

"Or you might simply think they're irrelevant," the doctor chimed in.

"Aaahhh—" Brandon groaned out loud, dismissing her with a wave as he stalked to the exit with me following suit.

"Do you have my mints?" he asked as he clattered down the stairs.

I handed him a pack over his shoulder as I tried my best to keep up with his long strides.

As soon as we exited the building, I began to rattle off, "Make-up has been waiting for you all morning. Your agent called to check if you had signed off on that photoshoot for Bonds next month. Jim called to ask if it was okay to move your weights training up to four this afternoon instead of three. Debra also mentioned that you needed assistance setting up a social media account so I can help you with that later."

I was still speaking as we both hopped into the black sedan waiting by the curb. "I got Germaine to prep you some breakfast. I wasn't sure if you'd had anything to eat yet." I rapped on the divider glass in the car. "Let's go, Lou!"

"Awesome." Brandon slumped in the seat, slipping his dark sunglasses on, and holding out his hand presumably for the food and I handed him the box from beside me across the way as the car drove off.

I was checking my phone to read new messages but the moment Brandon flipped the food box lid, he groaned so loud, I jumped in my seat. "What? What?"

He shoved the box back toward me. "I can't eat that. Who did you ask to make this?" he demanded. "Look, I have a very strict diet. I thought everyone was made aware of it. Do you think it's easy to stay looking like this? Take that crap away. I don't even want to see it."

Almost affronted by his accusatory tone, I pursed my lips. He was making it sound as though I had intentionally tried to do the wrong thing. But I took a deep breath to keep my patience in check.

For sure, I wasn't new to dealing with prima donnas. I was simply going to have to rise above and try to be understanding.

Today was probably a fluke. A rite of passage. A bad day. Surely, even Beyonce had one of those.

3

❦

Chapter 3 - A Personal Life

The administrative offices at *Lightscape* studios were about as tidy as the rest of the lot. It wasn't an unusual sight for the office to be busy even at night since production often rolled twenty-four-seven.

That evening though, there was only one laptop giving the room a soft blue glow and it was sitting on the PA's desk.

Among the precarious tower of folders, boxes of files, talent headshots, promotional materials, and half-empty containers of Chinese takeaways on the table, I had found a pile of papers just high enough for me to plunk my head on and have a snooze.

"Rye. Wake up."

Someone was shaking my shoulder.

"Rye?"

"I'm awake!" My head shot up off the table, almost sending the stack of papers cascading off one side. I blinked a few times to get my bearings before looking up with a wan smile. "Oh, hey, Victor."

Victor chuckled even as he surveyed the mess on my desk. "You okay, sweetie?"

"I'm fine," I murmured, straightening up my Bluetooth earpiece then gathering up some papers around my not-normally-this-messy desk.

"Is Lauren around?"

"She's with Debra working on a pitch."

"Oh. I'll just leave her a message then. Her phone's probably full of urgents." Victor reached for a Post-it note, leaning against the edge of the table to scrawl his message down.

I covered my yawn with my hand before automatically checking my phone for messages.

Victor regarded me with a sympathetic look. "So, how's it going?"

And I blinked up at him, considering how to respond.

Debra had asked me the exact same question at our "catch-up" that morning but I hadn't been quite sure how to describe the last two weeks.

"Nightmare" might have been an appropriate word, possibly "living nightmare."

It had been a whole two weeks of babysitting the most delinquent actor on the face of the planet.

What I had thought was a one-off bad day scenario quickly progressed into successive bad days with my cranky, self-absorbed, entirely entitled client. The job was almost akin to literally 'babysitting' in that Fyfe barely considered doing anything for himself.

Though to be fair, it wasn't that Brandon was necessarily rude to me in particular. He just seemed to enjoy sneaking off and making people go through hoops to get his time, taken to hiding in the oddest of places. I had even already added several new haunts to "Brandon's escapes" list for the record.

On the upside, I was already learning so much about the behind-the-scenes processes on a film set. I'd even made a few friends.

I was also thrilled that the production was for a cinematic fantasy television series, involving green screens, digital effects, and stunt coordination. Some days, I would get permission to watch the editing team or costume staff at work. It was endlessly fascinating how creative all these people were. I absolutely loved how everyone had such a vision of things.

That was on the rare occasions that Brandon showed up on time, or when I wasn't running around trying to instigate a manhunt.

Of course, I didn't tell Debra any of that.

Not that Debra wasn't aware of Brandon's antics.

I figured Debra wanted to get a feel for whether or not I was on the verge of quitting just as the ones before me had done. But it was just as I'd told Debra. I had everything under control. And by golly, I would.

I shook my head to dismiss the thought before meeting Victor's gaze steadily to respond to his actual question. "You know what? I think it's going to be okay."

A corner of Victor's mouth curled up in somewhat impressed amusement. "What are you still doing here anyway?"

"Research." I gestured to my laptop and Victor glanced over.

"Are you researching Brandon?"

"I just need a little more information about what I'm up against."

Notwithstanding everything I'd told Debra this morning, I couldn't keep putting up with the torturous days and nights for four more weeks.

I was down to reading every tabloid article, every news article, every footnote and mention of him in the media, every reference, every bit part, every role, every commercial in his past. I had to find a weakness, a smoking gun, some type of leverage.

I had to figure out a way to handle him. Otherwise, I was going to crack. And that was totally unacceptable.

I was sort of hoping to find something he was possibly allergic to and carry it around like kryptonite but aside from his fear of carbs due to his super strict diet, there was nothing else I could possibly use.

So far, I had found a couple of old girlfriends' contact information for potential blackmail, as well as I now had his mother's phone number on speed dial for emergency purposes.

My tone was resolved. "I won't let him beat me."

Victor chuckled again. "Somehow I don't doubt that for a second." He gestured behind him, motioning to leave. "Well, I guess I'll leave you to it. Don't stay too late."

My eyes lit up in alarm. "Late?" I checked my watch. "Oh, shoot." I sprang up and began gathering up my stuff. "I'm supposed to meet up with my friend for dinner."

"Oh, good." Victor nodded as though pleased at the irony. "You're still trying to have a personal life. Good on you."

I could only make a face as I watched him leave the room.

A blast of mariachi music washed over me as I pushed the door to the Mexican restaurant open. I spotted my friend Annie Benson waving wildly at me from one of the middle tables inside.

"Hey." I waved back as I wound around the tables to slide into the seat across from her.

"I'm kind of surprised you made it to dinner." Annie's brown eyes were wide. "I already ordered loaded nachos, but I was fully prepared to eat it all by myself."

That made me laugh. "Thanks. Anything's good."

"When you said you needed a place to crash three weeks ago, and I said you could move in with me, I thought that meant we'd be able to do girl's night sleepovers and binge-watch movies like in high school. But I've barely even seen you in two weeks."

I gave her a weak smile. "Yeah, sorry about that."

Tucking her black hair behind one ear, Annie tilted her head to regard me with a look. "Did you just come from work? That's what you wear? Jeans and comfy running shoes?"

I looked down at myself. "What's wrong with it? I do so much running with my job, it's not even funny."

"You haven't told me much about how work is going. Or should I even ask? You're obviously super busy. Is it awesome like you thought it would be? A lot of movie magic?"

"Well, the movie parts are awesome and fascinating. I just wish I could spend more time focusing on that instead of always doing errands, but I did make a friend in the editing team. Their work is so detail-heavy, it's amazing."

"I wish I could tell you interesting stories about my work but the most exciting thing that's happened this week is that the printer on Level 2 finally got fixed." Annie snorted her laughter. "You would think a building full of IT geeks could fix a printer sooner than three days."

Funnily enough, Annie and I had become friends when we were younger because we were both good with computers. Through the years, she had stuck to her passion while mine had somewhat deviated. But she was still my closest friend who lived on the west coast.

When the food arrived, Annie helped herself, scooping a pile of toppings straight into her mouth. She crunched as she went on, "Your mom called again. You know, I think I've spoken more to your parents than you have. You're never home to answer their calls.

I sank back in my seat. "I text them. They know I'm fine."

Annie shook her head. "I know your dad wasn't particularly happy about you leaving the job at the consulting firm last year."

I groaned. "I don't want to have that conversation. Why do you think I didn't tell them where I was going when I left? I'm an adult. I can make my own decisions. I don't need their disapproval or their guilt." I rubbed my forehead. "Besides, I have enough on my plate right now without having to worry about all that. Like today, I had to go to Chinatown just to find some specific dumb carb-free pork rinds, and then all the way across town to hunt down where a certain dry cleaner had moved, because—quote, they're the only ones who can touch his suits."

Annie made a face. "Oof. Brandon Fyfe IRL sounds like a nightmare."

I slammed my palm on the table, rattling the cutlery. "Yes! That's exactly the word I've been thinking."

"It's hard to believe for someone who overcame his crippling childhood shyness and coaches Little League every other weekend. Isn't that all true?"

"Oh, yeah." I shook my head. "Don't believe everything you hear. Fyfe even has some random write-up about his 'Five Books I Always Take on Vacation' in some magazine. But I can already tell you, he doesn't even seem to like read. The publicity people probably wrote all those because fans like that sort of stuff, to make actors seem more relatable, more real."

"Too bad. I always thought Brandon Fyfe was pretty cute."

I rolled my eyes. "That's beside the point. He's super irresponsible. He's never on time—oh, except for when fans mob him outside the lot to sign some boobs, I mean, seriously—"

Annie laughed. Her eyebrows rose eagerly as she propped her elbows on the table. "What kind of women does he like?"

"Oh, jeez." I made another face. "Any of them it seems. I think he'll flirt with anything even remotely female...or otherwise sometimes."

Annie smacked my arm. "Hey, do you think you could set us up on a date?"

Eyebrows snapping together, I smacked her arm back. "Shut up. You have a boyfriend."

"Tell Enrique that, would you?"

"What happened now?" I groaned. "I thought you guys were on for the long haul? Has it been what—four years?"

Annie sighed. "I don't know." She played with the bread sticks. "He's still avoiding the question about us moving in together, even though I asked him over a month ago. But I mean, come on. There's no harm in me browsing the current hot deals, is there?"

Wrinkling my nose, I pushed some guacamole around my plate with a broken nacho. "Only if you like them cranky, and self-involved. Besides, I'm not sure Brandon Fyfe dates normal people. He's an actor, remember? And according to his history, so far that I've read about or seen, he only dates actresses and groupie bimbos. He probably has a minimum of one plastic surgery operation."

Chewing on a mouthful, I stabbed a squishy tomato with a fresh piece of crunchy nacho. "Also, I wouldn't bet on him having a long life. If he keeps pissing me off, I might be more determined to bribe my yogi friend to formulate some belladonna to spike Fyfe's keto platter with, and permanently end that alleged problem he constantly complains about with his chronic insomnia."

Annie nonchalantly shoveled more food in her mouth as she spoke, "Alright, but let me know before you do all that, so I can erase all evidence that I know you just in case I'm suspected complicit to your crimes by association."

Laughing again, I shrugged in resigned mirth. "Come on. You know I would never do that. No matter how pissed off I am. I am a professional." I let out another long-suffering sigh. "I just wish Fyfe wouldn't waste everyone's time, not to mention our driver Lou's gas, with me having to constantly track him down every damn day of everyday *everyday*."

Annie perked up in her seat. "Hey, if you're having trouble tracking down your little actor all the time, I might have a suggestion for you." She wiggled her eyebrows, an ingenious glint in her eyes. "It's a new app from my tech team."

"No way, really?" I narrowed my eyes. "That would be perfect!"

And as Annie held out her phone to explain the features of her new app, I broke a grin, my spirits already lifting in triumph.

Brandon Fyfe was not going to know what hit him.

4

❦

Chapter 4 - Last Straw

I popped my head through the gap in the tinted glass door-way and spotted my client right away.

Magazine in hand, Brandon Fyfe was about to flop back into one of the comfy chaise lounge chairs in the spa lobby presumably to wait for his appointment, conveniently booked to avoid call time once again.

Stopping short, Brandon gawked in dismay. "Oh my god! What are you doing here?"

Grinning, I pushed the heavy door open all the way to come in. "Hey, Ian, I found him." I held the door open for Brandon's manager Ian Hollings to step through as well.

His gray eyes twinkling, Ian whistled. "That's some sharp tracking skills, Miss Williams." He shot Brandon a flat look as they approached. "Or you're getting lazy, dude. Seriously? The spa next door to the studio? Hardly a challenge."

"Or is it? You know, sometimes people overlook the ob-vious." Brandon's response was haughty. "I even thought I'd finally chosen the perfect hiding place this time, but you—" He shot me a glare. "I've barely sat my ass down. How are you finding me so fast anyway?"

I bit back a pleased smile. It was the third day Brandon had tried to duck out on call time. And so far, the third day that I had managed to find him in anywhere under twenty minutes.

Things were finally starting to turn in my favor. Thanks to Annie's miraculous app that I had sneaked onto Brandon's phone when he wasn't looking—which was always.

I merely grinned in triumph. "Irrelevant. Now get!" I pointed out the door.

Ian slung his arm around Brandon's shoulders. "Come on, now. The lady outsmarted you fair and square." He winked back at me.

My cheeks warmed. "Thanks, Ian." With an amused purse of my lips, I watched the two men walk toward the exit.

When I met Brandon's manager two weeks ago, I'd almost mistaken him for an actor too. Always in his tidy three-piece suit, Ian had almost the same striking build as Brandon. If not for the difference in their coloring, I reckoned the two of them could be mistaken for brothers.

Except Ian seemed more level-headed, mature, together. He wasn't exactly painful to look at either. If Annie were here, she'd probably be begging me to get set up on a date too. And, honestly, it didn't strike me as such a bad idea.

I shook my head to clear it. Glancing back at the counter, I bid the receptionist, "Please cancel Mr. Fyfe's appointment. Thank you," before following suit out the door.

The three of us started back for the studio compound. I couldn't help a little lightness in my step with my renewed sense of accomplishment and motivation—and maybe a tad bit of triumph. Instead of wasting my time hunting down Brandon Fyfe all the livelong day, I was finally actually making headway with my job.

Glancing back at me, Ian withdrew his arm from Brandon's shoulder. "I think it's fair to say that the days of you sneaking away from shooting are over now, buddy. So you'd better get your act together. In fact, I might be persuaded to assist Rye again next time you go AWOL."

I laughed. "Well, this was pretty fun. I'm sure I wouldn't refuse a next time."

Brandon walked ahead of us across the lot toward his trailer, his hands stuffed in his pockets. Not bothering to respond.

I met Ian's gaze as he fell back in step with me. "You know, I was curious about something."

Ian's smile was warm, open. "You can ask me anything."

Trying not to be flustered, I tilted my head. "I was just wondering why some actors needed both a manager and an agent." I gestured ahead to Brandon. "I mean, he obviously has both but some only have one or the other. Do you ever think maybe having both is over the top?"

Ian's face took on a thoughtful expression. "Well, I think having both is the best set up, really. Agents, I mean, their job is to keep you hungry. Find all the jobs, all the opportunities, book you up, fill your schedule—I think you might have noticed this with Brandon's agent, Davis—"

"Right, he sort of struck me as the type who would sell his own mother if it furthered Mr. Fyfe's career."

The two of us laughed again.

"I would say that's not too far off." His easy smile widened. "But a manager on the other hand," he added, "my job also includes making sure the client's well-being is catered for, ensuring their basic needs are also met. This way they can be more effective."

I nodded. "Oh, I see. So your job is sort of to take care of Mr. Fyfe. That's nice."

"I imagine it's similar to your job."

I blinked. "Me? No, I mostly run errands."

He gave me a look. "I'm sure you do more than that."

My neck burning, I switched the topic before I became completely flustered. "Well, I think you are really good at your job."

"Thanks. I think you are too." Ian's gray eyes were bright, lighting up his face.

Brandon had stopped at the door to his trailer, a sullen look on his face as he watched the two of us approach together. "Oh my god, are you guys flirting?"

Jumping in surprise, I flushed scarlet. "No!"

Jeez! Brandon Fyfe was going to ruin my chance with Ian before I even had one. Did he have to be so annoyingly perceptive? Also, *when* did he get so annoyingly perceptive?

Ian merely chuckled under his breath. When his pocket buzzed, he reached for his phone. "Well, I guess I better get back to work too. I'll see you later, Rye." He gave Brandon a short nod. "Later, Brandon."

Brandon waved him away without a word.

I climbed into the trailer behind him with a dejected sigh. I would have wanted to talk to Ian some more, ideally without His Royal Jerkiness around. But I guessed it was too much to hope that I might ever get a date this century. So much for that.

Holding my clipboard, I resigned to rattle off a few items from the 'Never Ending To-Do List'. "The office sent some merchandising samples. You're supposed to go through and approve them later."

But Brandon seemed to be on a completely different wavelength. "He's single, you know."

I blinked. "What?"

"Ian." He gave me a pointed knowing look before moving toward the back to get changed.

I checked a fresh surge of annoyance.

Great. And now my illustrious client was wanting to interfere even more.

Aside from the fact that I knew that already, I had absolutely zero interest in obliging him with his irrelevant tangents.

Determined to keep my focus, I went back to my list. "Okay," I dismissed quickly. "Did you go through the recommendations for gala invites that Lauren sent yet?"

His voice floated from behind the closed door. "No. I don't want to do that. So," he started again, "I'm assuming with the flirting just now that you are also single?"

Ignoring his question, I frowned as I made a note. "You *don't* want to attend the galas or you wanted to look through the invites yourself?"

"I don't want to do either," he quipped. "You know, Ian's a really straight-laced sort of guy. He takes his job very seriously. But he's probably way too busy to date."

Tamping the urge to roll my eyes, I read on. "Miss Paige's people wanted you to send her a bouquet of flowers before the red carpet tomorrow for the press."

"They know I don't do flowers, and even if I did, I don't want to." Brandon re-emerged from the back room dressed in black pants and a plain white shirt, an eager look on his face. "Hey, I bet I could put in a good word with Ian for you. Or did you think you could seduce him all by yourself?"

Still ignoring his tangent, I clenched my jaw. "Lauren moved your press release to Friday. Is that scheduled far away enough from your other commitments?"

"Tell Lauren to move it indefinitely." He regarded me with a bemused look. "I suppose Ian is right and you actually are good at your job."

"I am," I couldn't help my response.

Brandon cracked a smile. "I'll bet. Let me guess. Your last boyfriend couldn't compete with your dedication to your work? He was probably an asshole."

Wincing slightly, I took a deep breath. It was bad enough that he wasn't far off the mark regarding the reason why my ex-boyfriend Blaine and I had broken up, but it was something I was most definitely not wanting to get into right now. I went back to my list. "I've gone through some of your fan mail from last week and Debra said to pick a couple to respond to."

"I don't want to."

"Fine. Then don't." My frustration was quickly building into molten fury. I scratched the item off my checklist emphatically with a loud scrawling of my pen.

The phrase '*waste of time*' echoed in my head. It was a sentiment often used by Blaine. I was wasting my time, wasting my talents, my brains, wasting my education on this all artsy nonsense. Not surprisingly, the same sentiment was also employed by my parents, once or twice or many, many times. I had wasted time and money on a 'real' education—just to get a job picking up coffee for famous people.

Never mind that this job actually entailed undertaking a myriad of responsibilities including quite a lot of detail-oriented tasks, requiring a level of organizational capability that would shame an industrial engineer, but here I was, not even able to get to do all that.

Waste of time.

If Brandon Fyfe was just going to waste my time, what the hell was I even doing here?

I tersely read the next item on my list. "Scott said there's a message at reception from your girlfriend."

"Which one?"

I shot him an exasperated look.

Grinning, he crossed his arms behind his head. "What? Do you know how hard it is to keep all these names and faces straight? I don't even get any sympathy?"

The particular word struck a nerve.

The pretentious self-pitying plea in his eyes easily turned my mood sour. Ian was probably right. In terms of staffing, Brandon Fyfe needed as many people as possible to deal with his crap.

I swallowed hard. I had kept my patience in check for over two weeks, dealing with every one of my client's shenanigans, but instead of being grateful, here he was looking for the last thing someone like him should be getting.

It was enough.

A flush of anger heated my face, tightened in my chest.

I leveled a dark glare at him that must have been so dark, Brandon's cocky smile faded a bit. An almost gratified streak of pleasure coursed through me that he could read the change in my countenance.

He was so going to get it now.

"Sympathy?" I nearly growled as I tried not to scream, tried not to smack my clipboard in his big, fat, arrogant face. "Are you freaking kidding me? You are the biggest goddamn baby I've ever met! You only think about yourself. You complain about everything. You don't have any regard for other people's time and responsibilities." I sucked in a breath. "You have such an incredible job! An incredible opportunity to inspire millions of people around the world. But you take all that for granted! And all you want to do is whine about your stupid food platters and stupid mints and stupid fame."

Eye wide, Brandon's face had paled at my outburst, but I couldn't stop now.

It was a whole two weeks of pent-up fuming anger and helpless frustration.

And fear.

I was going to fail.

I was going to have to go home to my already disapproving family and swallow all the voices thickening with nagging because they had been right when they'd said I could never do this.

I had to prove them wrong. I absolutely had to make this work.

I couldn't let an upstart delinquent baby of a man like Brandon Fyfe derail my plans altogether.

Chest heaving in frustration, I rambled on, "Do you know that all I've ever wanted was to be part of this business? Even if everybody I knew was against it, my judgmental parents, and certainly my even more judgmental ex-boyfriend. I've loved movies for as long as I can remember and every single aspect of this whole process fascinates me! But if I have to be stuck with you, I think I'd rather clean toilets at a football stadium for an entire year. You are so freaking jaded, you suck all the enthusiasm out of this wonderful job, and I don't want to end up like you." I almost spat the last word out. "Now, stop screwing around and get the hell ready. They need you on the goddamn set."

I didn't bother to check his reaction. I stormed out of the trailer.

5

Chapter 5 - Renegotiation

I stared at the grinning faces of Brandon Fyfe on the two boxes of souvenir t-shirts by my feet. Somehow I had to get my client to approve the merchandising samples. I *still* had to work with my client for at least the next four weeks.

Sitting back in my seat, I closed my eyes for a moment, groaning in remorse.

Blowing up in his face and rambling on about my own hopes and dreams this morning was probably not the best way to get his cooperation.

Although to his credit, Brandon hadn't once acted like a prima donna since I'd last spoken to him this morning. Or maybe he'd been busy terrorizing someone else who hadn't been actively avoiding him all day.

I fully expected Debra to come screaming out of her office and kick me off the production for being entirely unprofessional. Could I possibly explain? Surely Debra already knew what dealing with Brandon Fyfe was like.

I was checking messages on my phone when the door to Fyfe's trailer slammed open. I sat up alert.

After a whole afternoon of shooting and intermittent breaks, Brandon Fyfe stepped out—late again. He was wearing denim pants, aviator sunglasses, and a leather jacket hooked in the crook of his finger was slung over his shoulder. A whole James Dean vibe going on. And it was totally working. A bunch of staffers were already looking over. Probably appreciating those tight jeans.

He paused mid-stride to fix his sunglasses. Standing in the middle of the lot, the setting sun behind his silhouette, he already looked so good that I could probably have shot an entire movie right then and there.

I shook my head briskly to clear it, as several visibly haggard people descended upon him like a flock of birds to usher him to make-up.

Walking on eggshells and being anxious about getting fired was definitely not how I wanted to spend the rest of four weeks in this job. But if Fyfe was going to be an asshole, he was going to get what was coming to him. And if nobody else on the crew was going to stand up to him, then I had no other choice.

I clenched my jaw, steeling myself for another showdown. Pushing up to stand, I followed the little retinue toward the make-up trailer and slipped through the door.

Having pulled off his sunglasses, Brandon sat in the chair, motionless as Victor and Helen fussed about, patting layer upon layer of foundation on his face as quickly as their hands could move.

Brandon was staring straight at his reflection in the mirror but his eyes were unfocused. It was as if he'd gone through these motions so often day after day, he barely registered what was happening any longer.

A melodious little Pitbull riff blared from the phone in his pocket.

He shifted to pick it up, mumbling the beginning of the conversation before his voice rose. "Yes, yes, I read the damn script." He ran his fingers through his hair. "I was just hoping the character would be more than two-dimensional, you know? What if we—?" He stopped short, possibly having been interrupted. "But it would be really nice to—" Interrupted again, he paused to nod. "I know. I understand." He rolled his eyes. "Give the people what they want, right?" He hung up the phone with a sigh.

I took that as my cue to interrupt. Clutching the two samples of the t-shirts, I sneaked around the chairs to stand by the mirror in front of him to make sure he couldn't ignore me. "Mr. Fyfe."

Glancing up, Brandon turned sideways slightly to ask. "What is it? Someone wants me to sign their chest again?"

I shot him a weird look then held up two sample shirts. "You're supposed to choose."

"Let's see—one of them has a picture of me and the other one has a picture of me, boy, that's a tough one." His forehead was creased in upset, his lips pressed tight.

I must have been staring at him.

"What?" he snapped.

I looked away. "Nothing." But glancing back at him after a moment, I considered the expression on his face.

Makeup hid the dark circles under his eyes really well but those blue eyes that were always so vibrant in photographs were dim and lackluster. And despite his shiny façade under the bright bulbs lining the mirrors, Brandon just seemed...tired.

It struck me at the same time that the sinking feeling in my stomach registered.

The truth.

Brandon Fyfe *didn't* want to be here.

Not only that, Brandon Fyfe would rather be anywhere else but here.

If I really thought about his behavior for the past few weeks—skipping call time, avoiding commitments, being instantly super cranky about every little thing, it was glaringly obvious.

Did everyone else know? Perhaps I was even the last one to find out. Nobody had told me anything. Then again, finding that out wasn't really part of my job. Or maybe had I been so focused on my own stupid issues, I hadn't recognized the signs?

The realization caught me off-balance for a moment.

Brandon sighed again, gesturing to the shirt on the left. "This one, I guess."

Snapping back to attention, I nodded. "Thanks." I set the shirts aside and chewed on my bottom lip, feeling somewhat uneasy.

"Ready," Victor announced as he and Helen stepped back, both seemingly breathless. Helen fussed with the tools on the table with a clatter as if to tidy up, while Victor gestured his arm toward the door to rush Brandon out.

I gave Victor a nod to indicate I was taking over to drag Brandon to the shoot myself. But Brandon didn't even so much as glance back at me as he fast-walked out the door toward *Stage 31*. Like he was upset or strangely motivated.

Whatever the case was, I needed to clear the air if I wanted to preserve a good working relationship, not to mention my sanity, if I wanted to keep this job.

I hopped a bit to try to get ahead of him, to get him to catch my eye. "Um, listen, Mr. Fyfe. I'm...so sorry I lost my head this morning." I put my hands up in defeat, sort of walking backward. "Honestly, how you do your job is none of my business. I don't need to understand or judge or analyze anything. I know there is no way I could possibly relate to whatever you're going through and I doubt I ever will or ever could. My job is to help you and that's what I'm going to do."

Brandon looked stunned for a moment. Pausing, he cracked his neck, and the darkness in his countenance lifted with a shadow of a smile. "Right. Thanks for that," he said. "It's just...it's a bit hard to be polite when you're hungry all the time."

My eyebrows lifted in understanding. "So...diets do make people hangry."

He gave me a deadpan look. "Do you know what it's like to be restricted to protein shakes and see everyone else around you gorging on jelly-filled donuts and fried freaking chicken?"

Despite myself, I couldn't help a laugh.

He smiled at my reaction, the sparkle almost returned to his eyes. "You know, I still remember the last time I had a chocolate fudge brownie. It was so moist and mouth-watering and it was just so..." he trailed off, closing his eyes as if in bliss of remembering, before letting out another sigh. "You probably already know, I only get one cheat day every six months. I have a countdown running."

The abject wistfulness in his eyes almost made my heart sink. I gave him a rueful look. "I'm really so sorry about the food mix-up last time. That was a rookie mistake. From now on, I will be more vigilant. I will personally go through all the food the caterers prep for you. I promise I'll be better."

Still with a hint of a smile on his lips, Brandon's gaze dropped slightly as though in deep thought. When he met my gaze again, those deep blue eyes nearly made my pulse race. For the first time, there was no trace of annoyance in it, and it was incredible how a mere look from him seemed to hold me in place.

I already knew he had that sort of effect on women. I had seen him do it over a dozen times in the past few weeks. But I had to admit, when it was directed at me, its efficacy was on a whole other level.

"Take it easy," Brandon merely bid before he kept walking.

Taking a deep breath to regain my bearings, my smile widened in relief.

At least I wasn't going to get fired.

Not today anyway.

6

Chapter 6 - Façade

"Turn it up, Shawn."

A delayed coverage news broadcast of the evening's awards show flickered on the TV mounted on the wall in the chaotic *Lightscape* studios staff room. Awards show nights for the company usually meant the entire staff had a bit of time off and everyone was rushing to take advantage of it.

Shawn, one of the publicists, was gathering his things together to get ready to leave. "You turn it up." He tossed Jillian, another PA, the remote control and it almost hit her in the face.

"Ow! Why did you have to do that?" Jillian whined.

"Children," Victor called from the table behind them, his tone teasing, "let's not be throwing things at each other. You'll end up in the hospital instead of the AVALON bar."

I chuckled. Clumsily eating my noodles with chopsticks, I leaned back in my seat to enjoy everyone's rare, easygoing energy in the room.

Lauren leaned against the table beside me. "Look at that." She gestured to the TV.

I looked up. "Look at what?"

The camera was following a couple of starlets of every shape and color on the red carpet with outfits ranging from wild to wilder to just plain bizarre.

Victor whistled. "Ooh, you just know that's going to end up on tomorrow's 'Red carpet Dont's'."

Lauren and I laughed.

"Well, I'll see you guys later." Shawn bid as he headed for the door.

Jillian jumped to follow. "Wait for me!"

The shot panned out to show the crowd around the carpet with the hundreds of screaming fans in the cool, crisp night before switching to the marquee again.

"And there's our golden boy."

The camera turned toward a sharply-dressed Brandon Fyfe and actress Zoe Paige who were pausing for a photo in front of the marquee.

Zoe Paige was another high-profile actress, whom so far that I had heard of was also high-maintenance in her own right. She and Brandon had been sporadically attending events together that it was enough for people to speculate about their relationship. Miss Flavor of the Month.

I had been exchanging messages with Zoe Paige's PA for the last few weeks but I didn't know much else about the actress yet. I folded my arms across my chest. "At least she's hot," I remarked. "They look great together."

"That dress looks like Versace," Victor guessed. "What do you think, Lauren?"

Lauren tilted her head in consideration. "What do I think? I think why is she bothering with that neckline? Everyone knows only J Lo can pull off that neckline."

"True." Victor gave her a practiced secret handshake which ended with a hair flip. "Though I would have liked Fyfe in that number from the last show, remember that?"

"What the shirtless tux?" Lauren quipped. "I know our boy's hot but, come on, that only ever looked good on Cha-lamet."

Victor chuckled, straightening up. "Anyhoo, Lauren, we'd better skedaddle before any of the higher-ups catch us here and we'll never escape."

Lauren rapped against the side of my desk. "You got any-thing planned tonight, Rye?"

Glancing around the now-near-empty office, I grinned. I gestured to the pile of letters scattered on my desk alongside a fresh batch of Chinese takeout containers. "Nah, I'll prob-ably just finish up here and then head home."

Victor made a face. "It's like one of the few nights we have off, Rye. Go do something fun. It's Friday."

"Sure, but someone has to go through all this fan mail, and guess what? It's not going to be our golden boy," I quipped ruefully.

Lauren was craning her neck to peer out the windows at the far end of the room. "Oh, jeez, I think a limo just pulled up. Victor, we gotta go."

Victor alerted and quickly grabbed his jacket, he shot me a grin. "Toodles!"

I shook my head in mirth. I slurped another mouthful of noodles before refocusing back on the pile of fan letters heaped on my desk.

Debra had insisted that Brandon respond to at least a couple so I had decided to take the initiative.

I hadn't even leafed through any more letters yet when Scott, one of the security guards, popped his head through the staff room door. His eyes lit up upon spotting me behind the desk. "Hey Rye, that was Fyfe's limo that just arrived," he announced.

"What?" My eyebrows furrowed in puzzlement. "He's back already?" I pushed my chair back to stand up, and with a sigh, I plucked a couple of fan letters from the mess on my table. "I guess it's time to get back to work."

With a resigned grumble, I strolled out toward the trailers. The lot was so quiet and isolated, it was almost creepy.

But I had been looking forward to some peace and quiet to focus on finishing up some tasks without any interruptions. With the rest of the staff gone, tonight would have been perfect.

Resisting the urge to smack myself on the forehead, I shook my head in remorse. I should have taken Victor and Lauren's lead and escaped the lot way earlier.

Approaching Brandon's trailer with the tinted windows, I couldn't see if the lights were on. I pulled on the door handle to check if it was still locked, but it easily slid open.

"Mr. Fyfe—" I called out as I climbed into the trailer before instantly stopping short.

My client was standing in the middle of the lounge.

My shirtless client.

"Oh my god, I'm so sorry!" I turned and put a hand up to block my eyes. But it was too late for the warm flush that shot through me from glimpsing the broad, smooth planes of his chest, those ridiculously well-defined biceps, that sculpted abdomen... Holy crap, I should have knocked!

Given the specifications of this job, I already expected there would be a certain lack of modesty but it was still a bit shocking all the same.

I wasn't a prude by any means. And it wasn't like I was secretly spying on him. I had to pull myself together if I was going to get my job done. I made a mental note to prepare for future similar instances, as I was fairly certain this wasn't going to be the last time I saw his bare chest in all its glory.

I shook my head to clear it. "Um, I thought you and your girlfriend were going to the after-party?"

Brandon's reply was dull already. "Wasn't feeling it. Also, Zoe's not my girlfriend."

I pursed my lips. "Funny that's not what *Hello* magazine said last month." I peeked up over my hand and furrowed my eyebrows to keep looking away. Brandon was tossing around things, possibly looking for the TV remote, but he was still not dressed. "Aren't you going to put a shirt on?"

"It's my trailer. If I don't want to wear a shirt, I'm not going to wear a shirt."

At the stubborn self-assuredness in his tone, I couldn't help a roll of my eyes. "Fine."

Well, of course. Brandon Fyfe was probably used to this. He *probably* had very little modicum of reserve left in his body. It only further supported my rationalization. It was me that totally needed to get a grip. If he didn't care, why should I? In the grand scheme of things, this was probably just another Friday for one of the hottest actors in the world.

I went to sit at the dining table, my back to him, and pulled up my phone to rattle off some messages. "Lauren said you absolutely have to do the galas. She also sent a list of charities for you to look at." I held up the envelopes of fan mail I'd picked out. "And here are those two letters that Debra said you should have a look at. I picked them at random."

"Are we still doing that?"

"Debra says jump. We say 'how high?' right?"

Brandon slid into the seat across from me. Fortunately, he had pulled on a dark blue cotton t-shirt—a form-fitting number that hid nothing at all, but still...

The solemn expression on his face seemed exhausted, withdrawn. He thumbed through the letters, his expression unchanged. "What do you think about these?"

I shrugged. Maybe he was sick of reading the same things over and over. "I think with social media and everything, it's inspiring that some people still take the time to send snail mail to their favorite actors."

He nodded, muted. "I suppose that's true."

I gave his appearance another once-over. I figured after bumping elbows with the who's who of Hollywood at the awards show, he was probably drained. "You're probably exhausted from the awards show."

Not responding, Brandon tapped the edges of the letters against the table top as if he was thinking about something. Glancing up after a moment, he met my gaze and put the letters down. "Do you want some coffee?"

I straightened up, alerted. "Oh, alright. The usual—double shot, half and half, two pumps of hazelnut?" I sprang up to leave but he caught my arm. I looked down at him. "What?"

"I was asking if *you* want some coffee."

I blinked, my eyebrows furrowing, and shook my head. "Um. Not right now."

He pursed his lips. "How about hot chocolate?"

I shot him another confused look.

"You know what, never mind." He got up, still holding onto my arm. "Let's go get some anyway."

7

Chapter 7 - Café Meet

I turned in my seat by the big window. The fifties-themed café in the production lot was nearly empty too given it was Awards show night, except for the barista staff and one of the security guards in the corner booth reading a newspaper.

Unable to help my puzzlement, I gave Brandon a frown over the mugs of hot cocoa with the pile of extra marshmallows on the side in a bowl on the table between us.

Brandon had one of the large mugs between his hands as if he wanted to keep warm despite him now wearing his leather jacket.

When he met my gaze, my eyebrows lifted in a prompt. "Um, what are we doing?"

He sank back in his seat. "Taking a break."

I tilted my head. "I'm not sure I have time for a break right now." I checked my phone again. "I have a list of urgents and Davis wants you to call him back for—"

"He can wait."

I blinked at his abrupt retort. "Okay..." I peered at his face. "*Are* you okay?" Looking him up and down, I frowned again. "Because if you're not feeling well, I'd need to call the doctor and get you booked in. Maybe Lauren knows one available this late—"

Brandon's shoulders shook with his chuckle. "Rye. Take. A. Break," he insisted, his tone firm.

I blinked again. "Um." I dropped my gaze, unable to help a chuckle of my own. "Sorry."

He gave me a nod in direction. "Breathe, maybe? Have some of that hot chocolate."

With a wry half-smile, I took a big, showy deep breath. "There. Breathing. Check."

Brandon merely cracked a smirk but he stopped nagging.

Sitting back in my seat, I looked around again. The nearly isolated café and production lot was so quiet for a change, it almost looked like a movie set in its own right. Even though in a few short hours, once again, the place would be crawling with busy, stressed-out people, I had to admit it was nice to be able to sit quietly for a moment and soak in the ambiance.

I was really here. Living my dream. I almost couldn't believe it.

With my gaze, I followed the golf cart that drove past the window with a load of props on a trailer behind it. I knew it was headed toward another warehouse in the back of the lot where even more movie magic was tirelessly being worked on.

Clouds swept past the darkened sky overhead. It wasn't cold enough to snow but it was close enough to Christmas for the air to have that certain bite. The café already smelled like pine and cinnamon.

I couldn't help musing out loud, "This almost looks like that scene from Season Two. When you were transported to that quiet, little English hamlet with the eerily deserted café."

Brandon stretched his arm across the back of the booth as he looked around. He nodded in agreement. "You're right." He made a face. "Not my favorite scene to shoot though. It was cold as heck."

I grinned. "I still remember my favorite part of Season Two, that scene just before the attack at the war college. Your line when you guys were stuck in the frozen wasteland and you were telling Betsy how you didn't even care what happened to everyone as long as she was safe."

Eyes lighting up in somewhat eager amusement, Brandon leaned forward slightly. He cleared his throat, a serious look coming over his face so he could recite, "I don't want to face a day in this world without you in it. I can't breathe without you."

I shook my head with just as eager a manner. "No, no, you said 'Nothing in my world works without you.'"

"What?"

"Uh-huh. I totally remember it." I gave a fervent nod. "That was a fantastic scene—great writing!" Pausing, I shot him a teasing look. "I mean, you sucked, of course, but *that scene!* The way the show depicted your devotion to

Betsy throughout...just wow, it carried the entire season, you know?"

Brandon laughed. He gave me a look with narrowed eyes. "You always memorize entire scenes from TV shows?"

Shrugging, I stirred my drink. "Just good ones."

"We did most of that shoot on location. Before that, I'd never even been to Ireland. Did you know they also shot some of the new Star Wars movies there? A place called Skellig Michael?" He drew his phone out of his pocket and tapped a few times before holding it out to show me some photos. "Have you ever been there?"

Shaking my head, I leaned forward to have a look as he swiped through the random scenery photos of a beautiful island and castle ruins. "Wow, those look amazing. Some of those look like the set of a few Sherlock Holmes episodes." I met his gaze in wonder. "Maybe you could go back there if you did something with those big franchises—Star Wars or maybe some version of Sherlock."

Brandon wrinkled his nose. "Are you kidding? I'd never get put up for something serious like that. All my roles are so...blah. They require no range whatsoever. This is why people think I can't act to save my life."

Registering his reticence, I pursed my lips. "Well, I was only teasing before. You're really not *that* bad."

Chuckling again, he clutched at his heart. "Oh, thanks, my harshest critic."

I laughed.

Leaning back in his seat, he shrugged. "Most girls expect, you know—Connell Rhodes. Fearless loner hero with a heart of gold. Of course, when you get down to brass tacks, it's just me, and the illusion quickly unravels."

"Ah, the Rita Hayworth of it all."

There was a curious grin in Brandon's quirk, perhaps appreciating that I understood the reference. "So you really took film history in college?"

"Yeah."

"Why?" His eyes were so wide in bafflement, I couldn't help but laugh again.

"I told you already. I love movies. I've always wanted to be involved in creating the magic behind the scenes. Imagine it. In just one specific shot of any film, there are already so many aspects that different people get to work on. And in the end, it suddenly becomes this complete, beautiful vision. It's amazing!" I gazed off into the distance. "I would love it if I had to be immersed in nothing else but this all day, and it would just consume me, take over my entire life."

He tilted his head. "In my experience, usually when you want something to consume you it's because you want to forget about something else."

I shifted in my seat. "I suppose I always felt like my life was missing something. I just want to do something that matters. Something I could be passionate about. Something I would eat, sleep, and breathe. And live. It seems like hard work, but rewarding, you know?"

Brandon watched me as I spoke. Still leaning back lazily, his gaze was kind of unnerving.

My cheeks flushed. "What?"

"Wow..."

"Wow, what?" I repeated expectantly.

He shrugged again. "Nothing. I just...envy you, I guess. I wish I could go back to when I thought this was all so magical."

I frowned. "You don't need to go back to do that. You just need to change your perspective. Pretend everything is new again."

"Pretend?"

I gave him a mocking look. "Isn't that your main job anyway? Aren't you an actor?"

He smirked to himself before lifting his mug to take a sip. "Perspective, huh? I like that."

I was surprised that he seemed to be taking my low-level PA advice on board. My smile widened at his easy-going openness. Not assuming his opinions were the only valid ones. Not criticizing my possibly small view of the world. I had to admit I wouldn't mind the next four weeks if it was going to be like this.

Glancing down to check my phone, I sat up in alert. There were already a handful of new messages and emails since I'd last looked. I quickly drained my hot chocolate and moved to leave. "Oh, we really must be getting back to work now, Mr. Fyfe." Giving him a prompting nod, I peered to see if he was done with his drink.

He met my gaze. "Call me Brandon."

8

Chapter 8 - Not News

Annie's blender, the loudest blender ever invented, woke me up with a start.

"Annie!" I covered my face with my hands in complaint. Still tangled in my blanket, I'd nearly fallen off the narrow couch.

But Annie merely gave me a sunny smile. "Good morning, sunshine!" She sampled the contents of the blender with a spoon and gave me a prompting look. "Wake-up smoothie?"

Grumbling, I got up to head for the bathroom to wash up. Having barely gotten two hours of shut-eye from working late last night, I was absolutely in no mood to tolerate her morning personality. Plus, as soon as I shook off the fog of sleep, as it always happened with me, my brain was immediately flooded with my list of things to do.

What were the odds that today was going to be a relatively calm, relaxing day at work?

"Your mom called me again and left a message this morning since you never answer her calls, but I'm not sure—oh, dammmmmn—" Annie stopped short.

"Oh damn, what?" I finished up in the bathroom and poked my head out the doorway.

Her smoothie cup poised halfway to her mouth, Annie's focus was on the screen of her laptop laid out on the kitchen counter, but her eyes were already wide with shock.

Frowning, I walked over to check. I peered at the Hollywood article on the browser and my jaw dropped at the headline.

Brandon Fyfe's secret late-night hot cocoa with unknown cutie.

I turned beet red. *What the hell?* Craning my neck to look closer, I blinked several times to make sure I wasn't hallucinating. But it was still there.

Those big bold letters were right above a photo of the studio's café window from last night with an almost artistically-captured shot of me and Brandon Fyfe, our heads leaned close together, cups of cocoa on the table before us.

Annie's big brown gaze met mine. "Was this last night? What actually is that? It's not a date, right?"

Squeezing my eyes shut in frustration for a moment, I let out a loud groan. "Can these stupid tabloids sensationalize it any more? Jeez! It wasn't secret and it wasn't that late."

"They called you 'cutie'. Is that a good thing?"

"If I was six, maybe."

Annie looked at the photo again. "Aww, you guys look like you're having so much fun."

I made a face. "What? No. He was just showing me pictures from his phone of the shoot in Ireland. It was totally not meant to be fun."

"Oh yeah, tell that to the stupid grin you have on your face." She wrinkled her nose. "I mean, they blurred out your face, but I can tell you've got a stupid grin. Heck, having hot cocoa with Brandon Fyfe, I would have had!" She threw her hands up.

"Shut up, Annie." I groaned again. "This is such absolute crap." I reached for my phone. "Now I have to get his publicist to release a statement. I can't believe people are making this out like it's a big deal. That was just a client and his dumb PA, people. It was a meeting. It was just about work!"

Annie reached over to plunk the blender in the sink. "How did that even happen? I didn't realize you guys held client meetings at picturesque Hollywood cafes over hot chocolate."

"It was his idea! Ugh." I wrote out a few text messages to a few people in frustration, my fingers tapping loudly.

Annie slurped her smoothie as she scrolled through her phone. "Oh, now it's all over social media too."

"What?" I groaned again. "This is like a nightmare. On top of my *current* nightmare!"

"You are not going to believe the hashtags trending right now. Good thing it wasn't the two of you at some bar having drinks."

I dismissed that with a wave. "Fyfe doesn't drink. He says his body is a temple."

"Ooh." Annie fanned herself. "I'd worship the heck out of that temple."

The look on Annie's face made me laugh. "You're ridiculous! Do you even hear yourself?"

****

I had spent most of the day firefighting on the phone with Fyfe's publicist and several newspapers and social media channels to clarify what was really going on in that photo, and afterward, there was a mountain of tasks and errands from Debra.

It was probably lucky I was too busy to bother with the gossip. More lucky, everyone else on set also seemed too busy to be bothered. I figured given Brandon Fyfe's infamy, this probably happened here all the time anyway.

Brandon himself had been busy with shooting. I hadn't seen or spoken to him at all yet either. It was honestly a bit of relief and I could just keep focusing on work.

Having just delivered a box of scripts to Lauren, I was rushing back toward the offices to file some paperwork. Hearing my name called, I stopped in mid-stride to glance over.

A little puff in his jaunty step, Victor was walking up to me. "Hey, Rye. We can't find Mr. Fyfe again. He's not in his trailer."

From Fyfe's schedule, I was vaguely aware that everyone had just taken a short break from shooting. Did my client disappear again? I rolled my eyes and pulled up my phone to check on the tracker app. "Alright, gimme a sec."

A curious crease on his forehead, Victor leaned closer to see. "Oh, my golly! You actually installed a tracker on Fyfe?" Eyes wide, he seemed impressed, if not at least highly entertained. "Does he know about it?"

"Of course not."

Victor burst out laughing. "Well..." He gave my shoulder a few thumps in approval. "You just earned a brand new level of respect from me, little lady."

I bit back a smirk. "He gave me no choice."

"By the way, I loved that trending hashtag this morning. What was it... #brandonsnewcinderella?" His grin tinged mischievous.

"Oh god, not you too!" My exasperated groan cut him off and I spun to leave but Victor fell into step beside me. "I thought nobody here cared about that dumb gossip. I mean you don't really believe that it was anything other than a professional meeting, do you?"

"Of course not, honey," Victor confirmed. "I know you were just working. But these papers will find anything to write about, you know? It's really for boosting subscriptions. So I wouldn't think too much of it."

"It's fine, I guess." I rubbed the bridge of my nose. "Mickey and I already spent all day shutting it down. Fingers crossed some other bigger scandal breaks out on social media. I mean what are the Swifties doing today, right?"

With a teasing smile, Victor put his arm around my shoulder. "Although, the two of you looked really cute together in that photo."

"Vic!" I pushed away in incredulous protest.

Chuckling, Victor put up his hands in resignation. "What? I'm just saying."

"Come on." I cast a furtive glance around to make sure nobody had heard. "Don't be ridiculous," I hissed. "Plus, you know, Debra would have my head. I even heard someone from set dressing recently got fired for asking out one of the ladies from the art department—I mean, just for asking. She didn't even say yes!"

"Mm-hm. Debra calls it an efficiency drain," Victor mused with a nod. "And didn't you hear about Fyfe's previous PAs yet?"

I gave him a wary glare. "What about them? I know they all left or something after like two weeks. But everyone I've asked so far doesn't seem to know why. Either that or they don't want to tell me." I chewed on my bottom lip. "Did he actually date them all and they had to quit?"

Victor shook his head. "Well, I'm sure Brandon didn't *date* them. Whether or not he slept with them, your guess is as good as mine." He cracked a grin. "At one point, we even had a pool going on this, right before Debra shut us down."

"What?" I couldn't help a laugh.

"Either way, *le* question, still up in the air. Although, I wouldn't put it past him—or those PAs. I don't know exactly what happened with them, but I *do* know they were nowhere near as capable as you." He winked. "I mean, even

Lauren was saying how big of a help you've been to her just last week. She said you make the impossible possible."

"Really?" My chest filled with warm pride.

"Also, just between you and me, I think you're really good for him. Help Fyfe work out those self-esteem issues."

I nearly winced in my incredulous startle. "Self-esteem issues?" I nearly spit out. "Brandon Fyfe?"

"Yeah," Victor replied with a shrug. "I think you're really good for his ego. Fearless enough to take him down a few pegs every once in a while."

Giving him another playful shove, I burst out laughing. "Okay, that's enough. This is already ridiculous as it is."

His grin remained on his face. "So did you find out where Brandon is?"

I frowned over my phone at where the GPS pin was located. "Oh. He's on set?" My eyebrows furrowed in confusion.

Then again, I had to admit it was potentially pretty clever since the set would have been the actual last place we would have thought to look.

9

Chapter 9 - Unexpected

Double-checking through the list of finished tasks on my phone, I walked onto the set a bit later. Greeting one of the sound technicians by the sidelines, I smiled. "Hey, Bill. How's Fyfe doing?"

Bill gave me a thumbs-up. "Last scene before we move on."

"Great." I glanced over to the elaborate stage that had been made to look like the ruins of a dark castle. Without the lighting, it only looked like stiff cardboard panels on a stage with fake bricks strewn about.

Brandon was standing to one side of the parapet. He was gesturing with one hand, script in the other, practicing his lines, his expressions kept changing. He looked up when the director called him over to give instructions.

Cracking a small smile, I adjusted my grip on the water bottle in my hand and leaned against the back wall. It was fascinating how sometimes Brandon Fyfe could be so professional. It was almost like he was a completely different person.

Keeping one eye on my phone, I half-watched them shoot the scene. Knowing all the show's themes, I could tell it was already a rehash of a storyline from an earlier season. I recalled the wistful look on Brandon's face last night. I almost felt like I could understand what he must have been feeling.

Brandon had been doing this character for years. No wonder he felt so stuck that he didn't want to be here anymore.

The clapper snapped me out of my reverie as the take finished.

With a haggard sigh, the director called out, "Okay, let's get that and move on to light the next scene. Great job, people."

There was a nudge against my shoulder. "Hey, you."

Looking up, my eyes lit up in recognition. "Oh, hi, Ian."

Cup of coffee in hand in his always-tailored suit, Ian's gray eyes were bright and friendly. "How's everything going?"

Brandon was shaking a couple of the other actor's hands walking off the set. He glanced over at me and Ian across the room, meeting my gaze for a moment.

I turned to respond to Ian. "Oh." I gestured to the set. "I think they just finished shooting this scene, so at least Fyfe will have a decent amount of sleep tonight."

Ian's lips quirked up. "I meant, how's everything going with *you*?"

"Oh!" Blinking in surprise, I almost laughed. "It's fine. It's all good." Biting my lip, I figured he was referring to the whole tabloid incident this morning. I supposed it was too much to hope that Ian hadn't read it at all.

Ian gave me a knowing look. "I already heard you and Mickey did amazing work with the spin. Mickey even said you wrote better press releases than he does. I hope you weren't too stressed out about it."

My cheeks warmed. "Oh. That. I'm just glad it's all more or less settled, but thanks. I really—"

"Rye! Come here," Brandon barked.

I almost jumped in my stance. "Oh." I gave Ian a sheepish grin and a small wave. "Talk to you later."

I straightened up and headed over to Brandon. Reaching out, I handed him his water bottle and a box of mints. "That was a good take."

"Thanks." Brandon took a deep breath. "What's next?"

I checked my phone. "You're supposed to go through some changes for next week's scenes. The updated script should be in your trailer." I gestured toward the stage doors for us to head to his trailer.

But he seemed to be looking at me expectantly.

I blinked at him. "What?"

"That article this morning," Brandon supplied matter-of-factly with a frown. He took another deep breath as if already steeling himself. "Listen, I'm really sorry. I wanted to find you all day to apologize. You're probably really upset. I mean, that's just—" He shrugged with an exasperated sigh. "It happens all the time, you know?"

I met his gaze. Brandon looked remorseful but mostly again, exhausted. I could imagine it must be pretty difficult or impossible to keep a private life with his kind of job. It was funny the small things regular people took for granted.

Like simply being able to go get a cup of cocoa without making tabloid headlines.

I waved my hand. "It's fine." I had mostly released all my pent-up annoyance with Annie and Victor already so there wasn't much left. Besides, Brandon seemed stressed enough.

He shot me a surprised, still wary look as if he was actually expecting the pent-up frustrated yelling. "Really?"

"It's not like it's not easily explained away," I rationalized. "Mickey and I already handled it with the press and everything. It's going to be fine."

Brandon cracked a grin. "You just keep surprising me every day, Rye Williams. I can never tell what's going on in that pretty little head of yours."

Before I could even get flustered over his most casual of remarks, Brandon spun quickly to walk away. Snapping to attention, I followed at his heels.

Almost automatically navigating through the darkened lot, I scrolled through the next batch of to-do lists on my phone and stopped short. "The Social sent through some interview questions you need to look at." I stopped in mid-stride. "Oh, shoot. I forgot those papers you were supposed to sign for that fundraiser. Ah dammit, I must have left them in my apartment."

Brandon noted over his shoulder as he climbed into the trailer, headed straight for the bedroom, "I'll do it tomorrow."

"It's *due* tomorrow," I pointed out with a frown as I followed suit, still trying to rummage in my bag one last time to make sure the papers weren't hiding in there. My gaze snapped up when the bedsheets rustled as Brandon flopped back into bed. "Hey, hey, don't go to sleep yet! You need to sign those papers right now so I can express them first thing in the morning."

"What? I need my beauty sleep. The talent needs to rest. Leave me alone." He grumbled.

I shook my head, kicking the foot of the bed. "Seriously, don't sleep! I'll just go and get the papers for you to sign. You'd better not be snoring when I come back."

Brandon made a face. "You want me to wait for you to go all the way home and come back?"

"Yes. I'll be back in ten minutes."

"Ten minutes?" He blinked in surprise. "What, do you have a trailer in the lot too?"

"No. My apartment is really close by, so come on—sit up and read a book, or a script, or something. Don't you dare fall asleep," I called out, already turning to rush off. "I'll be right back."

I had always found the location of Annie's apartment incredibly convenient. When I'd moved in a few weeks ago, I had even considered it a lucky twist of fate that Annie's second-floor walk-up was a mere fifteen-minute leisurely walk from the studios.

Of course, I was practically running down the tree-lined streets. My footsteps slapped on the pavement as the shadows from the street lights overhead shifted and moved as quickly as I did.

Victor mentioned Lauren had just praised me for being capable. I couldn't afford to let her down today. Not when this task could so easily be completed if I only hurried.

My skin was already thrumming with anxiety, but when I slowed down upon nearing the apartment block, the hairs on the back of my neck stood up in alert.

I thought I could hear footsteps in my wake.

The streets were dead quiet this time of night, and I'd never heard of much trouble in the neighborhoods this close to so much security around the studios, but I knew I couldn't be complacent about any danger in this city.

Swallowing hard, I quickened my pace once again. Glancing up at Annie's apartment's window, I frowned to see that it was still dark. Annie wasn't home yet. There was nobody there to help me in case I was being stalked by some random drunk stranger.

Shoot. I fumbled in my pocket for my phone or my keys or the little mace spray bottle I kept in my jacket at all times.

The footsteps crunched over leaves as though they were right on my heels.

Taking a deep breath, I stopped short, in the hopes that I would catch the stalker off-guard. Once I felt a tall presence right behind me, biting my lip in a bit of a panic, I thrust my elbow back against the person's mid-section.

There was a pained groan.

Gritting my teeth, I whirled around, intending to punch him in the face next, but my eyes popped wide in instant recognition. I almost tripped backward in shock. "Brandon—!"

Jumping in alert, he lunged to catch me before I fell. One arm sliding around my waist, Brandon tugged me against him to keep the two of us steady and upright. His other hand clamped on my mouth to keep me from yelling any more.

"Shh!" Brandon shushed, giving me a pointed look. "You want to trigger a fan mob or something?"

My heart was pounding in my chest. That freshly-showered scent was ridiculously intoxicating. Strong arms were wrapped around my back, his firm shoulders beneath my palms as I braced myself against him to keep balance. With his leather jacket unzipped, his skin was warm through his shirt, but also because my chest was pressed right up against him.

Brandon dropped his hand from my mouth. His deep blue eyes gazing down at me, that minty scent, my mouth instantly went dry.

In the dark, isolated street, the shadows on his face, his hair falling part way across his forehead, I struggled to blink away the forbidding image of Connell Rhodes from my mind.

Any moment now, the musical score was going to crescendo into an epic orchestral theme, with a swell of strings and brass to build tension and excitement...

<h1 style="text-align:center">10</h1>

Chapter 10 - Vivid

I shook my head to clear it. Jeez. I definitely had a way too vivid imagination. Swallowing hard, I croaked, "You can let go now."

"Oh." Brandon blinked and unwound his arm from around my waist.

Blowing out an exasperated breath, I leveled a livid gaze at him. "You idiot! What if I hit your face and you bruised? Debra would have my head. Then I would get sued. Do you know how much your face is insured for? Jeez!"

With a slight grimace, he clutched at his stomach. "You know, you got me really good right in the stomach."

My eyes widened. "Oh shoot, I got you in the stomach! I'm going to get sued! Do you know how much your *abs* are insured for?" I threw my hands up in panic. "What—what are you even doing here?"

Brandon put his hands up innocently. "What do you mean?"

"What the hell—did you follow me home?"

He shrugged. "I thought you were lying. Nobody's house is ten minutes away. Besides, it's late. It's not safe for you to be walking around the city by yourself."

I quirked an eyebrow. "You were concerned for my safety?" I gestured to his not-at-all-covert get-up. "What about *your* safety? You can't be sneaking around the city by yourself either." I spun to head down the lane to Annie's apartment building.

"Whatever. I'm fine," he mumbled as he followed behind me.

Pausing at the door I'd just unlocked, I gave him a glare of consideration.

He gave me a pointed look. "What, are you going to make me wait out here?"

Groaning again, I rolled my eyes. "Oh, for god's sake, fine, come in." I waved him through.

Coming up one flight of stairs, I led the way through the door and flipped the lights on.

Warm yellow light bathed our cozy, lived-in space. Annie had been going for some kind of bohemian aesthetic with the mismatched furniture adorned in colorful throws, eclectic cushions, and strands of fairy lights for ambiance. Her vintage wooden desk was in the corner, cluttered with stacks of papers, a couple of empty reusable coffee cups, post-it notes of code fragments, and passwords stuck on the bevels of two giant monitors.

I went straight for the kitchen counter. "Here it is." I picked up a folder sitting on top of a neat pile.

Brandon's gaze roved around as if he was taking in every detail of the space. The already small apartment looked even smaller around his imposing presence.

I darted quick self-conscious glances around to make sure that at least no dirty laundry was strewn all over the place. It had been Annie's turn to tidy up.

I was relieved for a moment that it seemed Annie had not shirked her chores this week.

Brandon had walked up to a set of shelves filled with knick-knacks, Hollywood souvenirs, and programming books full of colorful page markers. He tilted his head to peer at a glowing green miniature Borg cube Bluetooth speaker in seeming curiosity. "That's pretty cool," he mumbled as he flicked the head of a Darth Vader bobblehead.

Watching him, I cleared my throat quietly. Over the past few weeks, it certainly wasn't unusual for me to be alone with Brandon, but having him in my apartment was an entirely different, completely surreal matter.

"You know what," I declared almost too loudly, "why don't you just sign it here right now so you can go back to the studio?" I motioned him over to come toward the kitchen counter.

Straightening up, his eyebrows rose. "What, you're not going to walk me back?"

I made a face. "I'm not your bodyguard. Also, I didn't ask you to follow me home. Now, come on. You really need to get back to get some sleep."

He rolled his eyes as he walked over. "Fine. Got a pen?" He rifled through the first few pages. "Hey, can you tell them to make sure the donation goes to all the international drop-off points too? Last time, they only did it here and I want to make sure the money goes where it's really needed."

I blinked. "But don't you already support three of these charities?"

He shot me a narrow-eyed look like he didn't understand my question.

I blinked again. "I mean, of course, sure. I can definitely do that."

Given Brandon's reputation, I hadn't expected him to be so generous. I was pretty sure I'd heard that Brandon had spent his first paycheck on a diamond-studded tuxedo but perhaps I should double-check that.

Shaking my head briskly to clear it, I veered my thoughts back to my to-do list. "By the way, since that Twitter scandal broke a few months ago, I still need to set you up with another social media profile."

He groaned. "Tell me why I need another one."

"Your fans want more channels to interact with you."

"I don't need another channel for random strangers to criticize my acting range. I get enough of that from critics and tabloids."

"Debra says you have to at least try." I pursed my lips since I understood his hesitation. "Anyway, critics are dumb. They only like horrible, sad things. You need to give them a chance to highlight the good stuff you do, like this charity, or that time you did that out-of-the-blue hospital visit for those kids last summer."

Brandon didn't even seem surprised that I knew about that even though it hadn't been covered by the media.

I supposed I didn't want to admit that while I was re-searching ways on how to contend with him a few weeks ago, I'd also encountered so much positive stuff about him. At the time, I'd thought surely the news outlets were just exag-gerating, and that all the articles were completely made up in as much as fabricated good press was made up.

But tonight, I wasn't so sure.

Like I *did* read the articles, but it was like it hadn't really sunk in until just now.

As Brandon shifted his stance to finish signing the pa-pers, I couldn't help studying his profile. His wavy hair had fallen part way across his forehead again, begging to be brushed back.

Get a freaking grip, Rye.

He caught me staring and I jumped to announce, "I think you should wear a hat or something on your walk back, just in case. Let me just..." Walking over to the closet, I turned my back to rummage for a hat he could borrow. "You're lucky my roommate Annie isn't here. She would totally flip her lid if she knew Connell Rhodes was in our apartment."

Papers rustled as Brandon must have finished with the paperwork and I glanced over.

"Is this your bed?" He pointed at the single sofa bed in the living area. A pillow was stacked on top of a folded wool blanket. "You don't even have your own room?" He slumped into the couch, making himself comfortable. "There's barely enough space for one person on this."

"It's called poor communal living. It's not like I make six figures with this job."

He moved in his seat to adjust the pillows behind him. "I'm so beat."

"Hey, do not lie down there! You shouldn't even be here. Go back to your fancy trailer."

"So cold. I'm your boss, remember?" He sat up and began to sift through a pile of stuff on the coffee table. *My* stuff. A scattering of pens, postcards, worn notebooks, and a pile of papers.

I dropped a sports hat on the table before him. Arms folded across my chest, I stood by the couch. "Um, no. Technically, Lauren is my boss. Look, stop snooping around."

He grimaced at the hat. "You like the 'Silver Knights'? They suck."

"Oh, shut up," I snapped. "My friends, Annie, Enrique, and I are planning to watch them play Texas next week at The Arena. I'm so looking forward to it." I chewed on my bottom lip. "Now, are you done judging the place yet? You need to go. Tomorrow's going to be busy. We still have so much work to do."

A blue folder on the table caught Brandon's eyes. "What's this?" He flipped through the first few pages, his eyes widening in surprise. "Did you write this?" There was a tinge of fascination in his tone. "It's a screenplay for an office sitcom."

I grimaced. "Um, yes." I reached over to snatch the pages back but he held them away. "They're just ideas."

His forehead creased as he read some more. "This is really good. I didn't know you were a writer."

"Barely," I dismissed flatly. "Look, I just do that for fun in my free time." I was still trying to grab the papers from his hand but I couldn't quite reach. "Come on now. How about you put it down?"

Standing up again, Brandon raised the folder high above his head and gave me a mischievous grin. "How about you come and get it?"

I gave him a suffering look. I wasn't about to jump around him like a puppy, attempting to get the papers back. "How about you need to grow up?"

He mimicked my face in insolence then let out a low chuckle. "You know, you should give this to Nancy. She's always looking for good scripts."

I shook my head. "No, I saw the stack on her desk. She has enough script submissions to last her an eternity."

"Not good ones."

I groaned at his incorrigibility. "Would you please—*pretty please*—give me those back?"

Hiding the folder behind his broad frame, he gave me a firm look. "Only if you promise to show this to Nancy."

"Fine."

He narrowed his eyes. "Tomorrow."

"Next month," I countered.

"Next week."

"Fine!" I threw my hands up in exasperation.

Brandon's grin widened in satisfaction. "Done." Turning on his heels, he dropped the folder back on the coffee table and moved to leave. "I guess I better go before your roommate comes back and freaks out." With no hesitation or apprehension whatsoever, he lifted the bottom of his shirt to examine his abs.

My gaze was automatically drawn to his ridiculously well-defined six-pack.

"Looks like you didn't bruise me," he noted. Glancing up, he gave me one last self-assured smirk before he slipped through the doorway and out to the hall. "Good night, Rye."

Staring at the door closing, I had to catch my jaw before it dropped.

11

Chapter 11 - Cheat Day

I studied the story outlines on the whiteboards with a half-smile of wonderment while everyone else filed out of the meeting room behind me.

One of the show's assistant writers, my new friend Wendy, had gotten me permission to sit in at the writer's brainstorm.

My skin was literally still tingling from excitement. It was absolutely fascinating to just be in the same space with all the talented writers on the show bouncing ideas off of each other. All the creative juices flowing throughout the meeting were enough to inspire me all over again.

And once again, regardless of all the grueling torture I'd initially had to endure, I was so grateful to have been given this job.

This being the show's fifth season, however, I didn't miss that everyone seemed a bit less eager to try new things or think out of the box. I supposed Brandon wasn't the only one feeling that sort of fatigue.

On the whiteboard, the story outline was also interspersed with in-show photos of Brandon AKA Connell Rhodes. In every shot, he had either an intense or angry expression.

Tilting my head in thought, I struggled to recall if I'd actually ever seen Connell smile on the show.

A vivid image of that devilishly handsome smile before Brandon had left my apartment last night flashed hot in my mind.

That arrogant jackass. For sure, he had known exactly what he was doing. I shook my head to myself in derision as I spun to leave the meeting room.

Of course, I didn't tell Annie about last night. She would probably go crazy and insist on laminating the sofa bed just because Brandon sat on it.

I straightened up my shoulders in resolution. I was totally overthinking this. It was weird to think of famous people as real people, but then again, they really were. So, big deal, Brandon Fyfe had gone to my apartment. He probably hung out at all of his Hollywood friends' fancy apartments all the time.

But were we friends now?

Was it even possible to be friends with BuzzFeed's Hottest Leading Actor?

This is really good. You should give this to Nancy.

My stomach stirred as I recalled the seemingly genuine expression on Brandon's face when he'd looked through my screenplay.

I smacked my forehead with my palm. *Dummy.* Why on earth had I even agreed to pass my screenplay along to Nancy freaking Myers? I would seriously die of embarrassment.

Really, Rye? Brandon Fyfe gives you one compliment, and you would do anything he says?

Slumping back in the seat at my desk, I let out a long, slow sigh as I stared at the pile of folders on my desk.

I needed to focus on work. At the very least, I needed to do something else to occupy my brain sufficiently enough for me to stop thinking about those damn sculpted abs.

As if I conjured him with my thoughts, Brandon burst through the office door. "Rye!"

Blinking at my startle, I met his urgent gaze and an impending alarm threatened to make my heart pound. But Brandon's wide eyes seemed excited instead of stressed for a change, I was instantly curious. "Hey. What's up?"

A slow grin spread on his face. "It's cheat day."

I almost laughed. I couldn't help an identical grin. "Excellent."

I gave the dining table inside Brandon's trailer an amused look.

Boxes of donuts and pastries were stacked on one end, alongside a bucket of fried chicken, two large pizza boxes, and several other fancy boxes of food that I couldn't even identify. The delectable aroma of all the food filled the trailer.

My stomach almost gurgled in hunger.

Brandon had slumped back in his seat, already digging into the food. He moaned. "Oh god. Oh my god. Mmm...this tastes so good."

I laughed as I watched him devour some brownies straight from the foil tray. Coming around to sit across from him, I gawked into the box. "Double chocolate, nice. But don't you have a photoshoot next week?"

Brandon huffed. "I don't care. This is *my* schedule. My day. It's the photoshoot that's been delayed and rescheduled itself on the wrong day. Besides, as long as I hydrate and do fifteen minutes of cardio beforehand, I know I won't feel so bloated."

Catching a distinctively pastel blue box at the end, my eyes widened. "Ooh...French pastries." My one actual weakness. "Can... can I try one of those?" I pointed at the box of multi-colored macarons.

He laughed and pushed the box toward me. "I'm so glad you're here to celebrate this with me. Usually, I eat alone. It can be a bit depressing."

"Are you kidding me? You've even got glazed donut holes here."

"Gimme." He shifted in his seat, his mouth already open.

I blinked in surprise at his somewhat too-casual prompt. For a moment, my brain wanted to go through some lengthy manner of rationalizations. I'd only very recently figured that Brandon possibly considered me to be his friend. Perhaps a certain degree of formality could be foregone. But was that enough?

Either way, Brandon was already waiting. I figured it would end up more awkward if I hesitated longer. I picked an icing-covered donut out of the box and carefully held it toward his mouth.

Brandon leaned closer, his lips almost closing over my fingers. "Mmm..." He closed his eyes again, leaning back, looking deeply sated. "Heaven."

In spite of myself, the look on Brandon's face made me laugh. I had certainly been on more than one food binge with my own friends in the past. It was even a tradition. Who's to say this wasn't exactly the same?

"My friend Annie loves donuts," I relayed. "I, on the other hand, usually only save donuts for serious emotional emergencies."

"Aw, come on. I'm sure you could make an exception for today too," Brandon teased.

"Ah." My eyebrows lifted. "Let's just say I'm somewhat less eager to get all this sticky powdered sugar all over my hands."

Brandon watched me lick the icing off my fingers. Sitting up, he held out a chocolate truffle. "Here, try this."

I moved to take it from him but he held his hand away.

"Open your mouth," he coaxed.

The sudden timber in his tone wasn't lost on me, but again, Brandon's manner was still all too casual. Tamping down the urge to rationalize again on overdrive, I figured I had just done the same thing for him, so it probably wasn't a big deal.

It *shouldn't* be a big deal.

Swallowing hard, I leaned forward slightly and Brandon popped the chocolate inside my mouth.

But when he pulled back, his finger grazed my bottom lip. I had to freeze in my seat so as not to jump to my feet as shivers shot up my spine.

One corner of Brandon's mouth turned up. "Isn't Belgian chocolate the best?" Dropping his gaze, he focused on the box of candy between his hands.

"Um...yeah." Managing to get up slowly, I took a deep breath as I walked to the other end of the trailer, the luxurious chocolate melting in my mouth—somehow, inexplicably—not making me less jittery.

The trailer felt way too cramped. Either that or I was more hyper-aware of being alone with Brandon—which was ridiculous. I'd certainly never had a problem being alone with him in his trailer before.

Trying to settle my racing pulse, I studied a pile of polaroids on a shelf, a few randomly staged behind-the-scenes captures of Brandon with some of the cast and crew from the show.

Clearing my throat, I ventured a question. "So...didn't you want to go out with some of your friends tonight, maybe?"

"I don't really have many friends."

Brandon said it so offhand, but I glanced over, a frown of sympathy already on my face.

But he quickly went on, dismissing whatever note of despondence was in the air. "Anyway, if I went out, I'd just get mobbed. I want to eat my food in peace. And I certainly don't need a paparazzi shot of me devouring all this."

The comical look on his face made me laugh again, easing my earlier nervousness.

"Tomorrow dry toast and egg whites. But tonight—" He flipped open the box in delight. "Four-cheese pizza." His eyes narrowing somewhat from his own challenge, he shook his head. "Oh, I can already feel tomorrow's heartburn."

I gave him a reassuring grin. "I put a new pack of antacids on your bathroom shelf."

"Aww, you're such a good PA." He cast me a big smile.

I laughed yet again. "Why, thank you, thank you very much."

Brandon's mood was highly contagious. He looked so happy. And after all the weeks of seeing him cranky and troubled, even I felt a certain type of relief, like the weight on my own chest had lightened too.

Walking back over, I picked up his phone which I knew was hooked up to the Bluetooth sound system in the trailer. "How about some music?" I paused to make a face as I scrolled through his lists. "Jeez, are all your playlists EDM?"

The relentless thumping of a deep bass line pulsated out of the surround speakers, nearly rattling the trailer windows.

Brandon's eyes lit up. "Turn it up. Hey, I love this song."

The door whooshed open. "Is there a party in here?"

I glanced over and beamed. "Oh, hey, Ian!"

"Ian," Brandon mumbled through a mouthful of pizza.

Ian climbed into the trailer. "Ah, cheat day, of course. I almost forgot." He gave both of us a big smile. "I come bearing good news."

Brandon tilted his head. "I thought we were already celebrating?"

"Well," Ian relayed. "Your booking for the Late Late Show just got confirmed, so that's something else we can celebrate."

Eyed widening, I clapped. "That's great!"

Brandon made a face. "Not as great as these eclairs. I mean, come on."

I shot Brandon a curious look before meeting Ian's gaze. "Does he not like doing interviews?"

Ian moved to sit on the bench across from the table. "I'm sure Dr. Blumenthal has this phobia rooted in his very first interview fumble when he accidentally dropped a movie spoiler. I have a clip from that Nickelodeon interview saved on my phone for future blackmail purposes."

"Ooh! Can I see it?" I nearly jumped into the seat beside him to have a look.

Ian laughed at my enthusiasm.

"Oh, jeez, when are you ever going to delete that?" Brandon groaned in complaint.

"The producers weren't very happy with him," Ian told me.

I watched the video where a fourteen-year-old Brandon was talking about one of his first movies. "Aww, look at this little cutie in the Spiderman T-shirt. You were so adorable."

Still frowning, Brandon shifted in his seat with a huff. "Hey, I'm still adorable."

"If you notice, Brandon had a bit of a lisp back in the day," Ian supplied.

"Aw, man! Shut up." Brandon whacked Ian's arm.

With a highly amused chuckle, I held up Ian's phone. "Hey, can you send me a copy of this too? I may also need it for future blackmail purposes."

Ian's nod was eager. "Sure."

Grimacing, Brandon glanced from Ian back to me. "What the hell—who said you guys could team up to make fun of me? You are seriously so annoying."

Still grinning, I picked out a piece of chocolate truffle from the candy box and held it out to Ian. "Here, Ian. You should try this."

With a hiss of displeasure, Brandon shot me a searing look.

I almost recoiled at the stern look on Brandon's face. "What? What?"

Looking from Brandon to me and back again, Ian's eyes gleamed with mischief. He pursed his lips to give me a look of disapproval. "Rye, don't forget. We are the hired hands here. Brandon is the prince. We should only be serving him."

I rolled my eyes and popped the chocolate in my mouth. "Oh, of course, how silly of me."

Ian chuckled again before focusing back on his phone.

"What are you doing now?" Brandon asked, peering over.

"Ordering you at least one bowl of fruit and more bottles of water," Ian said. "All I can see right now is the amount of salt on this table. You're so going to regret this in the morning."

Brandon groaned. "You don't want to start anything with me right now, Ian," he feigned a threat. "Don't you remember the epic food fight of 2019?"

"You are so juvenile." Ian shook his head in disapproval. "Besides, I believe I won that round," he declared smugly.

"Oh, you so did not!"

The indignant look on Brandon's face and the defensive look on Ian's were all too much, I burst out laughing all over again.

12

Chapter 12 - The Mob

"Are you sure you don't need help with this?" Jillian gave me an expectant look. "Lauren said to use all the resources on hand. Didn't you just help Shawn write like all the scheduled publicity statements for the entire month too? You don't always have to do everything yourself, you know."

Winking, I gave her a dismissive wave as I hauled a pile of folders in my arms. "I can do it. Don't worry about me."

I had to admit, I was really getting into the groove of things at work. Even Annie was in disbelief at my enthusiasm to get to work this morning. It was still hectic, challenging, and oftentimes impossible, but I felt like I'd just gotten a fresh surge of motivation. I might've even said I was actually starting to enjoy this job.

Laughing, Jillian patted my shoulder. "Be careful, Rye. You're taking on so much, you're going to end up just like *you-know-who.*" Her voice lowered with her last word before she smirked and spun to leave.

Grinning, I went back to finishing up sorting files.

It was a running joke on set that Debra was a superhuman overachieving workaholic. But the way I figured, there were worse people to be compared to. All going well, I was going to follow in her very distinguished footsteps to fulfill one of my lifelong dreams.

As if on cue, the door to Debra's office slammed shut. It was so jarring, nearly everyone within earshot turned to look.

Glancing over, my eyes lit up to see it was Brandon who had just walked out the door. He was headed across the lot where I knew he was due for a shoot. I jumped to catch up to him.

"Hey," I piped up from behind. "I heard a rumor that Tom Clooney was going to be working on a project with Debra. Is it true? Did she say anything about him?" I couldn't keep the eager curiosity out of my tone.

Brandon gave me a brief sideways glance but kept walking. "I think he's executive producing something."

"Oh wow, I can't believe it!"

Eyebrows furrowing, the already displeased glower on Brandon's face darkened further. "You like that guy?"

I shrugged. "Sure. Why not? What's not to like? He's handsome. He's smart. He's so talented. He's a philanthropist."

Brandon rolled his eyes. "Boy, someone's standards are so generic. I seem to recall him not being so generous over press time when we worked together on those spy movies."

Almost struggling to catch up with his long strides, my eyes popped wide. "Oh my god, you've worked with him before! Would you introduce me?"

The glare he shot my way was so unexpectedly sharp, I winced.

Okay... Someone had woken up on the wrong side of his eight-hundred-thread count Egyptian cotton sheet-laden bed this morning.

I dropped the questions anyway. Nearing the set entrance, I passed him a box of mints and his water bottle as usual.

Without giving me another backward glance or word of thanks, Brandon stalked into *Stage 31*.

I blew out a breath as I hung back.

Brandon's mood was entirely baffling today.

I couldn't help a puzzled frown. After the past few days, I'd thought that Brandon had significantly lightened up. I supposed I had incorrectly assumed that we were going to start getting along better. But Brandon had somehow morphed back into his jerky self.

Then again, I supposed it was probably better this way.

Had I been thinking even for a moment that I could possibly be friends with someone of his reputation, his status?

It would be much better if I kept to the professional lines. Much easier and definitely much less confusing.

Walking past the parking lot barriers, I pinned some folders against my side with my elbow so I could respond to messages on my phone on my walk back to the tent.

"Hey."

Distractedly, I glanced up to see one of the paparazzi whom I recognized was always milling around the set. Usually, the paparazzi gathered in clumps, cameras at the ready to snap the day's million-dollar photo, but for some reason, this one guy had strayed away from the pack.

With a narrow-eyed look, he walked along the barrier as I passed by the catering tents. "It's you again," he called out. "It was you in that article the other day, weren't you? The café date."

I waved to dismiss it. "It wasn't a date."

A female tabloid 'journalist' popped up seemingly from nowhere, right behind the first guy. "Hey! Hey, who are you? Are you Fyfe's new girlfriend?"

"No. I'm his PA. Read the press release."

"His PA? Are you dating Fyfe?"

"No. Don't be ridiculous." I glanced up to see several more paparazzi coming toward them to see what the fuss was all about.

The woman thrust a mobile phone up closer, her arm reaching across the barrier. "Ridiculous? Are you implying Fyfe isn't your type of guy?" she bellowed. "GQ's Face of the Year isn't every woman's type?"

I winced. "What? I didn't say anything like that—"

"So, Fyfe *is* your type of guy?"

Almost stopping in mid-stride, my jaw dropped in a fluster. "What? I don't—"

Several cameras were now pointing in my direction. Nobody seemed to be taking any photos yet, no flashes in my face, but it was enough to make me catch my breath.

An arm slid over my shoulders to veer me away from the mob. I almost jumped in my startle.

Ian put his hand out toward the paparazzi as though to block them out. "No comment, please. Thank you," he called out in a firm, but respectful tone.

Looking up to meet his gaze, I blew out a breath in relief. "Ian, thank god." My heart was pounding in my chest.

He shot me a wry smile. "Word to the wise," he began. "Try to always stay at least fifty feet away from the paparazzi."

I blew out a breath. "I'll remember that." Even after dealing with all the tabloids for weeks, it was a different level of fear-inducing panic to have to deal with the paparazzi in person, most especially when their target was you.

Ian must have figured ducking into the set was the safest course of action. He maneuvered us to a spot behind the cameras to watch the preparations of the set being lit before shooting.

Brandon was standing off to one side of the faux New York alley set with his eyes closed.

I knew it was how Brandon got ready for emotional or intense scenes. I figured he must have been internalizing the exact scenario of the take, getting into character, slipping into his role.

When he opened his eyes again, I almost shivered.

It was no longer Brandon standing there, but Connell Rhodes.

The costume designers, being the incredible people they were, could portray so many things just by the mere texture of the fabrics, the layering, the subtle embellishments. And I couldn't deny that the rough, brooding look fit the man so freaking well.

The noisy chatter around us abruptly stopped, and when the director yelled 'Action', it was as if the entire set suddenly crackled with the crap tons of loads of charisma oozing out of Brandon Fyfe.

I could almost feel the heaviness of his back story from all the way across the room, the repressed hurt he held onto about his lost loves, his deep regret about his massacred parents which he carried on his shoulders, his raging fury against his enemies, his fierce determination to right wrongdoings...

For most of the past few weeks, I had always only half-watched shoots. I was mostly preoccupied with awaiting potential new messages on my phone. I hadn't really had a chance to really observe an entire slot of filming.

Obviously, I'd already had an idea of how good of an actor he was, but seeing it all up close was another completely surreal experience.

There were other characters in the scene, supporting cast, extras. But Brandon was completely mesmerizing. His presence dominated the scene, the set, the world. It was hard to look away.

When the director finally yelled 'Cut!', Brandon's posture changed entirely.

As if the character slipped seamlessly off of him.

Ian was peering at my face, possibly noting the awe on it. He leaned over to whisper. "He's really talented, right?"

I almost scoffed. *Understatement.* But I managed a nod. "Absolutely."

As though Brandon sensed we were talking about him, he glanced over and noticed me and Ian by the sidelines.

When Brandon met my gaze, I actually had to catch my breath again. Some of the intensity from the shoot was still there in his eyes—indignation, displeasure. I couldn't even move.

I was, for sure, supposed to go do about a million things on my to-do list, go back to tiresome, endless work, but that mesmerizing look transported me to another time and place altogether.

I was back in that dark street the other night when Connell Rhodes—no, when *Brandon* had caught me when I tripped. The mere memory of how firm his chest was, how strong his arms were around me, threatened to flush my cheeks.

The cameras were all off and they weren't shooting, but again, it was as though Brandon's mere presence dominated...*absolutely everything.*

The strobe lights flickering overhead snapped me to attention.

Brandon had gone back to talking to the director.

Alerted, Ian looked up. "Oh, is that the time? I have to pop away for a meeting."

"Sure, see you later." I gave him a small wave as he exited the set. Then I moved to sidestep a couple of people rushing.

Looking around, I frowned. There suddenly seemed to be way too many people bustling on set, packing up and leaving, or setting up new things.

I caught one of the camera guys nearby. "Hey Joe, what's going on?"

"Oh, they're closing the set to shoot the shower scene next."

My mouth went dry. "The...shower scene?"

"Yeah, it's a fan service. They always have a scene where he showers."

Joe said it with a slight grumble so nonchalantly. I figured everyone was already sick and tired of doing the same thing over and over again, but I struggled to stop my jaw from dropping once again.

I had already seen him shirtless and there was no way to un-see those abs. I had to find another task that didn't require me to gawk at his bare chest all day. I'd better go back and check with Lauren to see if I needed to do more of her bidding.

But first...

I bit my lip and looked around *Stage 31*. The weather was getting colder and colder.

I hurried toward the offices again. I was pretty sure there were some first aid kits in the break room pantry. Opening the closet, I fetched what I needed and sprinted back to set.

Finding Brandon's chair on set behind the cameras, his robe slung across it, I slipped the heat pads into both pockets.

Surely, if Brandon got pneumonia because of that ridiculous fan service scene, it wouldn't be good. No matter how much of a jerk he was, it *was* my job to make sure Brandon was kept comfortable, right? I was doing this for Debra too, for everyone.

Not wanting to overthink what I was doing, I rushed to leave again.

Chapter 13 - It's Hollywood

"This is incredible, Stewart," I breathed as I watched the dual screens displaying timelines of footage from the shoot.

The small editing room already buzzed with creative energy, jam-packed with computers lining the walls, shelves overflowing with tapes, hard drives, and cables.

Stewart adjusted some audio levels from the control panel on the desk before him and clicked through to replay one segment of the video a few times over.

"I love this part." I gestured to the screen closest to me where the camera transitioned into a zoom-in shot while Connell Rhodes ran down a dimly lit street in a burst of fog.

"Oh, Fyfe complained about that damn fog all day," Stewart mused with a chuckle. "I almost thought he'd get the SFX guys fired and we'd never hear the end of it."

Amused, I tilted my head. "Really? I didn't hear about that."

"Surely, he must have asked you to demand Debra to put a stop to all the fog in the show."

I laughed. "Well, he hasn't yet."

Stewart narrowed his eyes. "If memory serves, Fyfe will take any opportunity to put in a complaint about every little thing in the show every day of the week."

"It could still happen." I wrinkled my nose in thought after a moment. "I guess, now that you mention it, I actually haven't heard any complaints from Brandon recently—or anything for that matter." In truth, I had been preoccupied doing Lauren's bidding for the last few days, I'd barely even spoken to Brandon.

Stewart's eyebrows shot up in surprise. "That's odd. I thought he couldn't last a minute without all that dedicated personal attention."

I chewed on my bottom lip, puzzled at this realization. "He didn't used to." I pulled out my phone to double-check my lists. The last thing I'd had to do for him was well over thirty-six hours ago—which was an oddity in itself. Like if I didn't know any better, it almost seemed like he had been avoiding me altogether.

"Did you piss him off or something?" Stewart asked offhand, his attention turning back to his monitors.

"What?" I frowned. "No way." But my brain went into instant overthinking overdrive. What could I have possibly done wrong? I automatically rehashed the last few days in my mind to analyze what I could have done that may have offended my client. Had I not been paying enough attention to Brandon's tasks? Could I have forgotten something important? Impossible.

I shook my head. "I mean..." I rationalized with a dismissive wave. "You know, he's a really busy guy. They're trying to finish up this shoot ASAP. Surely—"

Someone cleared his throat loudly by the doorway.

I blinked up in surprise upon seeing the figure leaning against the wall. His arms crossed over his chest in that charcoal sweater made his shoulders look even broader than they were. "Brandon!" I swiveled around in the chair. "S-sorry. Am I late for something?"

Brandon shook his head. "No, no." He cast a glance around the room full of monitors, his gaze settling on Stewart. "I was just walking by and saw you two in here. Uh...what are you doing?"

My eyes brightened. "Oh, Stewart was just showing me the dailies. I've always wanted to see the inside of a cutting room. I mean, this is where the magic happens, isn't it?"

His forehead creased a bit and his voice carried a tone of suspicion. "What kind of magic?"

Stewart gestured to the panel boards. "Editing."

Brandon blinked. "Oh."

I watched him curiously. Then I jerked my thumb back toward Stewart. "Stewart's going to show me some camera tricks next. Unless...well, did you need something?"

Brandon met my gaze. "Actually. Yeah."

I looked around as Brandon led the way up the stairs from one of the staff rooms. "I didn't even know there was a sitting room up here."

Brandon cracked a grin. "It's one of those things you know when you've been here as long as I have."

Leaning over the banister in wonder, I watched the tops of people's heads as they shuffled around the tables beneath them. "This is a great space."

I could still hear the muted chattering and laughter but the upstairs sitting room was relatively quiet and cozy. I had to admit that on some level, I was glad I didn't have to be alone with him in his trailer again.

With Brandon being so surprisingly self-sufficient for the last few days, I realized I hadn't even been alone with him since 'cheat day.'

Brandon set some folders down on the table before slumping into the plush couch at one end of the room. Was he about to tell me off for something heinous I might have done that I wasn't aware of like Stewart guessed?

Although Brandon didn't seem as cranky as he usually did. With any luck, perhaps his mood had returned to relatively stable.

"Is...everything okay?" I ventured as I walked over.

Brandon's bright smile was automatic, rehearsed. "Sure." Sitting up, he gestured for me to sit on the couch and picked up one of the folders.

I peered at the papers as I walked over. "What are those?"

"It's for an audition that I need to practice." Brandon held out the folder to me. "Would you run lines with me?"

Settling on the couch, my eyes widened. "Can I do that?"

"Sure. It's easy." He shrugged. "It's really more for me to get a handle on the timing and the reaction, so all you really need to do is read."

Rifling through the pages, I nodded. "I guess I can try. What's the role?"

His eyes shone. "It's for this technological suspense series. It's set in the future and I'm playing a spy from this alternate dimension. It's pretty gripping." He gestured to a page. "Let's start here. Just follow my lead." He cleared his throat and began to read.

He got into character so quickly, I flustered before snapping to attention, but I managed to read the next line for him. We volleyed lines back and forth for a few minutes before Brandon broke character. He stopped to nod. "What do you think?"

Blinking in awe, I returned his nod. "Wow, this does sound pretty cool." I flipped a few more pages to read on. "Though I wonder why they didn't start with this action scene and maybe did some sort of flashback instead? It might have had a stronger effect." I waved my hand dismissively. "Maybe, I don't know."

He stopped to think about it before giving me an impressed smile. "I think you're actually right." He blew out a sigh. "Either way, at least, this one has a fuller character arc than what I'm doing now. There's really not much else to Connell Rhodes after the fifth installment to this franchise."

I wrinkled my nose. The wistfulness on his face almost made my own stomach sink. "What would you really like to do?"

For a split second, Brandon looked surprised at the question.

Had nobody ever asked him that before?

His jaw clenched in determination. "I want to do something completely different. A more challenging role." His eyebrows furrowed in thought. "Maybe even a sitcom, like a comedy."

I had to stifle my sudden burst of laughter. "Comedy? Really?"

"What? I can be funny," Brandon noted with his chin up. "It's just there's so much more depth to those characters. I mean the emotional range of a regular sitcom is just intense, and you still get to do so much physical stuff, comedy, action. I think it would be amazing."

The light in his eyes brightened his entire aura. It was difficult not to be just as excited, difficult not to want to root for him too. "So, why don't you? Audition for a sitcom, I mean."

Brandon shrank back with a groan. "Come on. Everyone's pegged me for this broody, cheesy action-hero type. It would be a hard sell."

I grimaced. It struck me as strange for Brandon to put himself down. "Are you being serious right now? How on earth could any kind of 'Brandon Fyfe' be a hard sell? I'm sure even sitcoms would allow fan service shower scenes." I cracked a mischievous smirk.

Brandon's face crumpled. "Ohh..." I almost thought his face turned a shade redder than normal. He shook his head. "Tell me you at least didn't watch that."

Huffing, I gave him a pointed look. "Hey, I am way too busy with work to watch all your fan service shoots."

Brandon's chuckle rumbled in his chest. "That's right. I...wanted to thank you for the heat pads. That was you, wasn't it?"

My eyes lit up, almost feeling self-conscious. "Oh, that. No problem. I mean, you're welcome. I hope...you didn't get too cold."

He let out another sigh. "Give the fans what they want, right?"

"I guess..."

Tilting his head, he gave me an amused smile. "So, you're not too bad with the reading lines. Ever thought of being an actress?"

"Oh! No. Never. I'm more of a behind-the-scenes type of person. Watching what you go through every day, I don't think I could ever handle it. Not so much the acting part, but the 'everything else' that comes with it. The bad press. The gossip."

Leaning back in his seat, Brandon could only nod silently in agreement and somewhat resignation.

I was still shaking my head. "Like the paparazzi mobbing me the other day just because of that dumb café article of us."

Brandon shot up in his seat so fast, I blinked in a startle.

"What?" His eyebrows snapped together in a frown of instant concern and alarm. "A-are you okay?" He looked me up and down as though paparazzi harassment would have sort of external physical indications. His face full of remorse, he ran his hand through his hair in frustration. "I'm so, so sorry."

Surprised that he seemed quite concerned, I shook my head again. "It's fine, really," I assured. "Besides, Ian came over and helped me."

"Ian?" He visibly swallowed. "Man, that guy is everywhere, isn't he?"

His question was more of a displeased mutter, my eyebrows knitted together. "Is something wrong?"

Brandon met my gaze for a moment before looking away, his jaw clenching again.

I bit my lip. Jeez. Maybe he really was upset with me.

But there was a storm in his blue eyes, as if he was pondering something truly complicated, and growing more frustrated at the conflict.

For some reason, I couldn't bear his frown. That heavy cloud that had always seemed to hover over his head was back. When he didn't speak for a few more minutes, I peered at his face. "A frank for your thoughts."

Almost automatically, Brandon responded, "In America, they'd bring only a penny and I guess that's all about I'm worth."

I laughed. I supposed I shouldn't have been surprised how easily he'd caught on. "I'm willing to be overcharged. Tell me."

With a slight smirk, Brandon gave me an approving nod. "Casablanca. Nice."

I beamed, almost in gratification at having diverted his mood. "Ah, the man knows his classics. What's the next line then?"

Stopping short, Brandon gawked at me. "Seriously. You're testing me?"

"Yes."

"Me. Seriously?" He gestured to himself.

"Yes, you." I gave him an elaborate wave.

With a deadpan look, he warned, "Dude, don't test me on the Bogey."

I couldn't help a chuckle, my eyes glinting in mischief. "Aha, so you accept my challenge. Come on now. What's the next line?"

Brandon cleared his throat then affecting a nonchalant expression, he leaned forward to recite, "Well...I was wondering." His eyebrows rose in an expectant prompt, an unspoken challenge in retaliation.

I tilted my head. I wasn't about to back down. Casablanca was my most favorite movie of all time. "Yes?" I spoke softly, trying to mimic Ingrid Bergman's character's cadence.

"Why I'm so lucky, why I should find you waiting for me to come along." Brandon chimed in with the next line.

I broke another grin. "Why there is no other man in my life?"

"Mm-hm."

"That's easy. There *was*. He's *dead*," I exaggerated my recitation then struck a pose like I'd hung myself.

Brandon let out a laugh, but nonetheless was able to deliver the next line, "I'm sorry for asking." Pausing, he cracked a diffident smile. "I forgot we said no questions."

"Well, only one answer can take care of all our questions..." Trailing off, I was about to yell 'cut' and applaud to end the scene. But when I met Brandon's gaze again, those blue eyes were pinned on me.

The intensity in his expression held me still and my smile faded. Even as he was sitting a good few inches away on the couch, his presence, his warmth reached out to envelop me.

It was as if he'd chosen to remain in character. Bogey aside, I couldn't help being mesmerized. I'd felt the same thing the other day—in fact, every other day whenever he looked at me. And it didn't help that I knew exactly what happened next in the Casablanca scene.

And it seemed Brandon did too.

When he spoke again, he did so slowly, "And then...she kisses him."

The mere notion of kissing *him* sent shivers up my spine. Not even willing to blink, I swallowed. "And then he...kisses her back."

Brandon didn't move an inch but he was studying my face. His forehead creased in the slightest manner possible, his gaze dropped to my lips for the briefest of split seconds.

I couldn't move. Didn't want to move.

Was he actually going to kiss me?

Surely, he knew the effect he had on women. Brandon was just so beautiful. Broad and strong. His blue eyes, deep and dark. Those perfect cheekbones. His often unruly blond hair fell across his forehead—*again*.

How could anyone be in my position and not want to jump him right now? My heart pounded in my chest when I couldn't help my gaze dropping to his mouth too.

His lips looked soft and red.

Oh dear god, I was wondering what they tasted like.

Just then, Brandon slid backward in his seat, snapping to alert. "Um."

Wincing at his sudden movement, I jerked back to sit upright. I was already almost breathless. My chest heaving, I had to do a quick mental shake. What the hell was I thinking?

I pushed further away on the couch. "Oh, look at the time," I announced as I stood, belatedly realizing there were no clocks anywhere around. I pulled my phone out. "I mean, Lauren—I need to do—I have stuff I need to do for Lauren."

Brandon sank back into the couch with a small nod.

I tried to tamp down a grimace. "Um, good luck with your audition," I bid as I moved to leave.

"Hey. Rye."

Tentative, I turned around to meet his gaze again.

"Thanks."

Brandon's slow smile seemed sincere, I couldn't help returning it.

"You're welcome."

14

Chapter 14 - Distractions

Chewing on my bottom lip, I fiddled with a knot of scarves before tossing them onto the pile of clothes on Annie's already messed-up bed.

"A photoshoot?" My friend echoed, her brown eyes wide. "Tell me it wasn't for underwear."

I gave her a flat look. "Oh, yes."

Clasping her hands together, Annie squealed, crumpling the sweater she was holding. "Oh, mama, next time, can I please pop around and say I'm visiting you?"

"I didn't even want to be there myself!" I threw my hands up.

It was frustrating enough relaying to Annie the events of yesterday.

It had been one of those more challenging days.

For some reason, Brandon had been in no mood to shoot. Which made the photographers cranky. Which was made worse because the caterers were late. Which was made worse since the set was too cold. Overall, it had taken a significantly longer time than usual to finish.

After so many days of almost having a relaxing time at work, I was suddenly thrown into the deep end once more with hissy fits, tantrums, stress, and, heaven above, I didn't even know how it was even possible, but the shop had run out of Brandon's mints!

I had managed to get a different brand as a substitute, but I knew that wouldn't fly for long, so I had been in the studio back room, racking my brain, searching the web on my phone for anywhere in the world that might possibly deliver at the shortest notice ever, when—

"Rye!" Brandon's voice sailed out from the set just outside the door.

Already annoyed, I'd stopped short, rolling my eyes. "Brandon, for god's sake, there aren't enough mints in the world—" Except when I'd looked up, my jaw dropped clear past the floor.

Brandon had walked in wearing nothing but black fitted boxers—the kind that barely left anything to the imagination. Every inch of him was tanned and toned, from his broad shoulders to his long legs. He freaking already looked photoshopped. He was so *hot* it almost hurt to look.

I'd had to shake myself to regain my bearings—*and* snap my mouth shut.

I had to shake myself again to drag my stupid brain back to the present where Annie's still wide eyes were like laser beams boring into my skull.

"And what did he say?" Annie's prompt was eager.

"Nothing." I shrugged on the little black dress Annie insisted that I try on. "He just wanted to make sure I told his agent Davis that he was never going to do another one of those shoots in the middle of freaking winter."

I almost hadn't heard him. He'd pulled on a plush gray robe straight after but how else could I possibly have thought about anything else? I'd seen his underwear ads before—in huge giant billboards on buildings and shops. Of course, I had. But now that I had seen nearly all of it in the flesh, I couldn't quite get the images out of my mind.

I was extremely relieved and grateful that I was finally allowed to have this weekend off work and have heaps of time to *not* think about it.

Annie and I were supposed to be getting ready for the game later, but my mind kept wandering. My face was already heating from the mere recollection. "I can't stop thinking about his chest. He was so freaking beautiful. Annie, help me!"

Anne burst out laughing.

"I swear to god, if I see Brandon's bare chest again, I will literally jump him. There is no army on earth that can stop me jumping this man."

"I thought you hated him?" Annie asked between wheezes.

I bit my lip. "I don't *hate* him."

Which was wholly ridiculous.

Brandon may have been prickly at the start. In the last few weeks, I'd seen him deal with an inordinate amount of pressure—granted with more grace at certain times than others. He could still occasionally be an egotistical ass, but after commiserating in his disappointments, listening to his dreams, I had to admit I certainly didn't hate him.

I supposed I could say I liked him as a person—that was, now that I was aware he was actually a person and not just a shiny reflection of his huge ego.

I shook my head briskly to clear it.

Focus.

Turning to one side, I made a face as I surveyed my appearance in the mirror. The hem of my dress had a bit of a flare, stopping just above my knees, and if it wasn't for the black lace across the top, the neckline was way lower than I normally wore. "Are you sure about this dress? Isn't it a bit too much for a hockey game?"

"Are you kidding? It's perfect." Shaking her head, Annie tossed some more clothes onto the bed for her to choose from. "Besides, girl, only one thing right now's going to help you."

"What?"

"You know, a good old-fashioned booty call." She winked. "Why don't you actually call him and go scratch that itch?"

My mouth went dry. "That's...the dumbest idea I've ever heard." Still, a shiver of thrill shot up my spine. But I shook my head to clear it, to regain some semblance of reasoning. "Debra has a very specific and very strict rule against dating in the workplace. She would have me blacklisted from anything even remotely production-related. I'll never be able to show my face in Hollywood ever again. Plus, I also heard she might even have connections to the mob. It's super unprofessional to date the talent."

Annie blinked. "I didn't say 'date' him. I just meant do him. Have it all done. Get it all out of your system."

"Okay, *that* is the dumbest idea I've ever heard," I amended, waving the topic away. "Besides, you're making it sound so easy. Brandon's not interested in me that way. He's a big hotshot actor. He's got hundreds of hot actresses drooling all over him."

"Even better," Annie pointed out. "That means he's totally used to women coming onto him." She tilted her head. "Come to think of it, you've been working with him for a while now. I thought Brandon Fyfe hit on all his previous PAs."

"Honestly, I don't know what the hell is wrong with him." Shrugging, I moved to the dresser as Annie waved me over to the mirror to fix my hair. "For a supposed rampant playboy, he's certainly playing it cool. I swear to god, he almost had a clear opening the other day when we were..." Again, my face flushed already. "Reading Hollywood lines."

"And?"

"And he didn't."

"He didn't make a move?" Annie's eyebrows rose. "You're kidding."

"I am not." I gave her a flat look. "I totally embarrassed myself making up a lame excuse and virtually had to run away." Groaning, I covered my face with my hands. "I was such an idiot. How could I have ever thought someone like him would be into me anyway? Even with his super low standards, I still don't make the cut."

"What on earth are you talking about? That's just nonsense. He'd be insanely lucky to have you. Maybe he was just busy, or stressed, or maybe there's something else going on, another girl maybe."

I fiddled with the loose jewelry on the dresser. "Whatever. I just need to make sure to avoid any more awkward situations. It was lucky I had to run errands the other day, so I didn't have to watch when they shot Brandon's fan service shower scene."

"A shower scene?" Annie squealed and tumbled back in bed with a sigh. "You're killing me!"

"Focus, Annie!"

Annie propped herself up on her elbows to give me a look. "Oh my god, jump him. Jump him right now."

"Annie, I'm being serious here."

She threw up her hands. "So am I. That is definitely an option."

I groaned. "I can't!"

Nearing exasperation, Annie huffed. "Then control your damn self!" she proposed. "Or quit that job and go home to Long Island. Admit to your folks that you made a big mistake coming here, that you should have stuck to that highly respectable consulting job, making money hand over fist whilst your soul slowly dies..." She put the back of one hand against her forehead accompanying a dramatic sigh.

"Thanks a lot," I drawled, tossing a plastic curler at her. "Some help you are"

Blowing out a breath with a laugh, Annie shot up from her bed. "Alright, fine!" She walked back up toward the dresser. "In that case, what you need is a good distraction." Her eyes gleamed once more as she began to comb through my hair. "Which is perfect timing because Enrique said Steve was going to come with us later."

I met her gaze in the mirror. "Who's Steve?"

"Enrique's friend from work. He's coming with us to the game."

"Oh, okay."

"And he's pretty cute."

I stopped organizing the mess on the dressing table to turn to glare at Annie. "What?"

"What?" Annie gave me an innocent look.

"Annie Elaine Benson, are you seriously trying to set me up with some guy again?" I narrowed my eyes.

"You *just* said you couldn't stop drooling over your boss." Annie threw her hands up as if to rationalize. "I'm offering you an alternative! If you can't get with Brandon, why not get with Steve?"

"He's not my b—" I stopped short when both of our phones started buzzing.

In fairness, Annie's phone only went off with one text message while mine had gone berserk buzzing with message alerts one after the other.

"What on earth—?" I picked it up and my frown was instantaneous. "You've got to be kidding me."

Glancing up from her phone, Annie craned her neck. "What?"

I groaned, straightening up. "There's some kind of emergency and Debra's in San Francisco. Sounds like a mess. I have to go to the set right now."

"Right now?"

"Apparently." I sighed.

"Perfect timing!" Annie noted. "Enrique's just arrived downstairs with Steve. They wanted to hang out before the game, but I'll text him that you have an emergency and they should drive you to work first."

"Drive? It's like ten blocks to the studio."

"Rye! Just let the men drive." Annie gave me a pointed look. "Besides, I still need to get ready." She started absently brushing her face with blush.

I rolled my eyes. "Fine. I'll text you when I'm done so you guys can pick me up to go to the game, okay?" I grabbed my jeans from the edge of the bed to get changed.

"Don't." Annie stopped me and pushed me toward the door. "You'll be late. Besides, you look gorgeous. Show Steve some of them moves."

"Moves? What are you—?"

Annie draped my bag over my shoulder, put my mobile phone in my hand, and opened the door for me, nudging me out of the apartment before I could attempt any further protest.

15

Chapter 15 - Last Minute

I sprinted across the studio lot, cursing my high heels. At the very least, I should have insisted that Annie let me change back into sneakers before I'd left. Though I was belatedly grateful to her that I hadn't had to run all ten blocks in said heels.

Enrique was perfectly happy to drive me to the studio.

And Steve was perfectly happy to meet me, it seemed. He was also quite impressed to find out what I did for a living. He was looking forward to catching up and hearing stories about my work at the game later.

I could tell Enrique had been enlisted by Annie to drop so very many hints about Steve's wonderful personality during our conversation. In all honesty, Steve seemed like a nice, decent guy, and he was pretty cute. I really couldn't fault Annie's matchmaking choices.

But I couldn't think about that right now.

Lauren's latest text message said that Brandon had gotten into an accident while shooting some stunts, but she didn't say how bad it was or whether or not he was fine.

My heart pounded in my chest as I headed for his trailer where the GPS said he was.

How bad could it possibly be?

Surely, the studio had safeguards in place to prevent serious injuries, right?

Brandon had to be okay.

Before any more horrors of worst-case scenarios could play out in my head, I pushed open Brandon's door. "Brandon?" I almost leaped into the trailer.

Brandon was slumped on the couch in the living area, watching TV. "Oh, great, Rye, you're—" The words seemed to die on his lips as he glanced up.

Slightly out of breath, I met his gaze warily. "What?"

Brandon had stopped short, his unhurried gaze traveling from the top of my styled hair, to the little black dress, to the bottom of my four-inch heels in an open appraisal and then all the way up once more until he met my gaze again.

I flushed under his prolonged heated gaze. It was clear from the expression on his face that he liked what he saw.

It looked like he wanted to say something too but after a moment, he just averted his gaze.

"Umm...are you okay?" I fidgeted nervously on my feet. "Lauren said you got hurt doing stunts. Where are you hurt?" I assessed his appearance but a cursory once-over didn't tell me anything. At least, he didn't seem to have any terribly visible injury. "Which stunt did you do? Was it the parapet one again? I thought you'd finished shooting all the castle ruins scenes. Also, I thought your stunt double Ricky was going to do the rest of the stunts instead of you. Wasn't that what you agreed with Debra last month when you almost fell off the mounted glider?"

Brandon made a face at my barrage of questions. "One at a time, please! I still have a headache."

"Sorry." I made a face again. "Well, I'm here now. What do you need?"

Still frowning, he cleared his throat and waved me over. "Help me get up. I have to send some kind of memo." He set the TV remote down. "I told them it wasn't serious. I just sprained my back and I need a couple more ice packs. But they're making it out like it's the end of the world."

At that assurance, a wave of relief washed over me and the tension in my own shoulders eased. "Probably because Debra isn't here," I noted. "I'm sure everyone is sworn under pain of torture to make sure nothing bad happens to you while she's away."

Coming closer, I slung his arm around my shoulder and braced an arm around his torso. I tried to ignore how firm his muscles felt beneath my hand. He was just so solid...and warm...

As he stood, Brandon's nose brushed against my hair, likely by accident, but the deep rumble in his throat seemed on purpose when he spoke, "Why do you always smell so good?"

I froze. "What?"

He looked away again. "I mean, I guess you didn't run all the way here, did you?"

"No, Enrique and Steve drove me," I replied as I helped him hobble over to the table.

"Who?"

"My friend Enrique. Annie's boyfriend. Remember I told you about them?"

His forehead creased even as he nodded. "Who's—the other guy?"

I blinked. "Oh, Steve? I think he's a friend of Enrique's," I replied, steering him toward a seat.

Brandon braced his hand on the edge of the table to sit himself down. "You don't know him?"

I shook my head. "Not really."

"Not *really*?"

I shot him a strange look. "No. Why? Do *you* know him?"

"No." He gave my clothes another once-over. "Were you going on a date?"

I shook my head. "Not a date. Just some of my friends going to see the game I mentioned last time, remember?"

His face turned mocking. "That's what you're wearing to a hockey game?"

Puzzled, I looked down at myself. "What's wrong with it?"

Brandon's face crumpled further. "Nothing. Doesn't matter," he muttered.

Already exasperated with his petulance, I sat down across the table and pulled out the laptop to make notes.

When Jillian burst through the door, I almost jumped. I figured she was probably meant to cover for me today while I was on leave.

"Mr. Fyfe—oh, sorry, hey, Rye, you're back!" She swept her frizzy hair out of her face as she came on board. "Um, I just thought I should tell you that Miss Paige is here. She pretty much just stormed through the front door."

Groaning, Brandon sank back in his seat. "This is the last thing I need today. Can't you just—?" He flicked his hand in a shooing motion.

Jillian turned those wide eyes to me, her expression turning pleading. I supposed she didn't feel confident enough to confront a big Hollywood A-lister actress herself.

Unable to help a begrudging sigh, I pushed back up. "Fine. *I'll* deal with her."

Jillian shot me a huge grin. "Thanks, Rye. You're the best!" Before she spun on her heel to exit, she paused in mid-stride as if remembering something. "Oh!" She gave Brandon a bright smile as she set the clipboard of instructions on the table. "Mr. Fyfe, the P.T. will be arriving shortly too, and you're scheduled to leave for the Late Late Show in a few hours. Lou will bring the limo around. Are you sure you don't need me to come along tonight?"

"Yes—I mean, no," Brandon amended quickly. "I need Rye to come with me."

I blinked. "What?"

He tilted his head with his drawl. "I mean, I'd go alone, but...I'm not so sure I feel all the way better from my injury." As if to make his point, he rubbed his back with a grimace.

"You did say Debra wanted to make sure nothing bad happened to me. You wouldn't want to get anyone else in trouble while she was away, right?"

Cringing, I closed my eyes for a moment and took a long, deep breath. "Fine. Fine!" I threw up my hands before snatching the clipboard up as I made my way to the door. "Rye will do everything, shall I?"

Jillian beamed at me as I passed her before following suit at my heels.

"Thanks, Rye!" Brandon's airy self-satisfied voice sailed out just as the doors shut.

I spotted Zoe Paige stalking down the lot from yards away. I tugged on Jillian's arm before she slinked away like a coward. "Hey, can you at least please make sure everything's ready for Mr. Fyfe's interview tonight?" I hissed close to her ear before I let her go.

"Aye-aye, sir." Jillian mocked a salute before skittering away.

I quickened my pace to make sure I met up with Zoe halfway, somewhere not too close to the barriers and the paparazzi, but she bumped into my shoulder as she passed me—likely, on purpose.

"I'm here to see Brandon." Her curt declaration seemed to imply she didn't need to elaborate.

Hissing under my breath, I spun around to block her away again. "I'm sorry, Miss Paige. Mr. Fyfe isn't receiving visitors at the moment."

Zoe's perfectly-shaped eyebrow shot up. "Visitors? I'm not just a visitor. I'm worried about him. I heard he got hurt."

"He's fine now. He just needs some rest—hey!" I squeaked when she tried to push past me. "Miss Paige, please calm down!" Almost in disbelief, I gripped Zoe's shoulders to nudge her back. The woman was insane! Didn't she realize the paparazzi were right there?

"Calm down?" Zoe put her hands on her hips, her volume indicating she likely didn't care at all if the paparazzi were watching. She gave me an assessing look up and down. For a moment, I was glad I didn't look like a gopher wearing my usual ratty clothes. "Who are you to tell me to calm down? He's not your boyfriend!"

I clutched the clipboard to my chest with a fresh burst of confidence as I stared her down. "With all due respect, Miss Paige, he's not your boyfriend either, okay?"

Zoe's face turned red. "What do you know?" she screeched. "You're just his PA!"

"I know quite a lot actually," I replied. Dropping my voice, I motioned to lead Zoe away. "Now, I'm sure neither one of us would really rather spend all of tomorrow spinning this story for the tabloids, so if you would please—desist?" I made sure my expression was imploring instead of annoyance.

That seemed to snap Zoe out of it, her eyes clearing. Darting glances around as though finally aware of her audience, she straightened her shoulders.

I broke a relieved smile. Tentatively putting a hand on her shoulder, I gave her a slight nudge so we could both walk away. "I think you could use a drink, Miss Paige. Shall we?"

But Zoe shrugged me off with a huff and stomped toward the studio offices herself.

Heaving another exasperated sigh, I rolled my eyes as I moved to follow suit. Walking toward the studio offices, the paparazzi's questions shot at my heels one after the other.

"Did you girls just have a fight over Brandon?"

"Were you two ladies fighting over Connell Rhodes?"

"Was Zoe jealous about your café date?"

"What's your name? Are you really just his PA?"

With another huge sigh, I shook my head. Jeez. So much for tomorrow's headlines. But all I could do as I walked past was put my hand up. "No comment, please."

16

Chapter 16 - It's My Job

A few hours later, after having completed all the paperwork and other last-minute tasks, I waited by the side door of the studio beside the limo that would drive us to the Late Late Show. I tapped my fingers on my clipboard.

Annie had told me on the phone earlier that Steve was more than a little bit disappointed that I wouldn't be able to join them at the game. But Annie herself seemed quite thrilled that I was going to be able to watch a popular live talk show. Apparently, it was imperative that I took candid pictures of all the celebrities I came across tonight.

Taking a swig of my bottled water, I frowned at the new email notification that dinged from my phone.

ATTN: URGENT rider update – FYFE

I wiped my mouth with the back of my hand and clicked into the email to read through it, only to stop short at the first two items.

1. French pastries from Louis Sergeant.
2. Flat screen, internet enabled. Note: Sports subscription.

What the—? I furrowed my eyebrows in puzzlement. But before I could read through the whole list or mull over what it could have possibly meant, Brandon finally sauntered out of the *Lightscape* studios office.

For some reason, Jillian was tiptoeing behind him and nodding, as though he was giving her instructions. She sneaked a glance up at me before giving me a little wave and disappearing back through the door.

Impatient to get this all over with, I moved to open the limo door. I eyed Brandon's plain jeans and sports coat with a critical eye. "Is that what you're wearing to the interview?"

Brandon gave me a flat pointed look. "Of course not. We need to pass by Balmain's on the way to pick up my suit."

Oh dear lord... I groaned inwardly.

Balmain's was an elite clothing shop that served mostly celebrities. And it was all the way across town. We were going to be stuck in rush-hour traffic forever. It was a good thing the Late Late Show was true to its name.

Brandon's gaze went up and down me. "You changed."

I shot him a look. "Of course." I wasn't about to wear a cute dress and heels to run around doing errands all night. Fortunately, I always had several spare changes of clothes at the studio for emergencies. For one thing, my feet were definitely glad to be back in sneakers. "I wasn't aware I needed to be in formal wear to watch a talk show from backstage."

"Couldn't hurt."

I knew he was being facetious but I caught him grimacing a bit as he bent to get into the limo and I winced too. "Are you sure you're feeling up to this? I mean, you just had an accident today."

Not stopping, he cracked a smirk. "I love that you worry about me."

I scoffed in incredulous disbelief. "Shut up." Still shaking my head, I slid into the seat across from Brandon's and shut the door.

Brandon inspected the cuffs of his jacket. "The show's studio is right near my apartment. Tell Lou I need to swing by to pick up a couple things after the interview."

"Sure." I knocked on the divider to quickly give the driver instructions before we drove off.

Brandon cast me a look across the way. "By the way, thanks for dealing with Zoe earlier. I was watching from the window." He looked inexplicably pleased.

I made a face. "Oh, god, please don't remind me."

"What? That was quite impressive. I know for a fact Zoe Paige can be real bull-headed when she wants to be." He cracked a mysterious grin. "And I wanted to thank you..." Reaching over, he pressed a button on the side of his seat and a large panel behind me crackled to life—and loudly.

I turned my head. "What the—?"

A large flat screen was installed at the front. The TV was currently showing clips of a chilly glassed-in rink, thousands of screaming fans waving flags, and about a dozen guys rumbling around on skates amidst a flashing scoreboard with the colorful stats.

NHL National Hockey League
Dallas Suns vs. Silver Knights

Brandon peered at my face. "You said you didn't want to miss this game, right?"

I gave him an astonished look.

"Here." He handed me a box of pastries and stretched out in the leather seat. "Now, isn't this even better than that stuffy stadium? I bet not many stadium suites have this level of first-class service." He reached over to open the mini fridge installed in the car, drew out a couple of root beer bottles, and offered one to me.

I stifled my laughter as I looked around. The email I'd gotten was making a bit more sense. "You set all this up."

"Jillian helped." Shrugging, his eyes glittered in mischief. "Hey, contrary to what you might think. I'm not such a bad guy," he confessed. "I didn't want to totally ruin your night."

"Oh, but you wanted to ruin it just a little?" I quipped, my eyes narrowed.

He didn't respond, except for the self-satisfied grin that spread across his face.

Charming.

God help me. That was the word.

Brandon's smile was so freaking charming.

He gestured beside him. "Sit over here so you can watch it better."

I felt like a walking contradiction.

I followed Brandon as he led the way through the private entrance of Balmain's fancy-schmancy clothing boutique. With the crystal chandeliers, Avant-garde décor, stiffly uniformed staff, and distinctly-fresh scents. Up the stairs was a brightly lit gallery-slash-dressing room with shiny little tables laid out with complicated canapes and sparkling champagne on ice.

My stomach was in knots, possibly from my nerve-wracking anxiety, but at the same time, my pulse was racing from the thrill, the excitement.

Was I even working right now?

I was having way too much fun for this to really still be work.

Back in the car, watching the hockey game with snacks, cheering the teams, futilely trying to spot Annie and the others in the crowd, or yelling at the ref's calls, regardless of what the call was, it almost felt like I was just hanging out and having fun with a good friend—even if it was Brandon.

Or I really didn't want to say it. I didn't even want to think it.

It sort of felt like...we were on a date.

When Brandon glanced back at me as if to check if I was still behind him, that smile again on his face sent a shiver up my spine.

I shook my head to clear it.

Only one of the snobbish staff gave me a narrow-eyed look down her long nose, but it was enough. Maybe it was fine in the car. It was safer. But right now, I needed to put my PA hat back on. And like, pretend I never took it off to begin with.

Miss Long Nose rolled a rack of suits for Brandon to browse through, toward the half-circle white leather couch, while a few attendants went to check the canapes and champagne one last time before they all disappeared back down the stairs.

I checked my phone, but there was nothing. I supposed everyone knew I wasn't supposed to be working today. No new messages. No new emails. Nothing remotely urgent to preoccupy my thoughts otherwise from the fact that Brandon and I were virtually alone again.

"I gotta say it's a bit liberating to know Debra isn't here to boss me around," Brandon remarked with a grin as he thumbed through the suits.

"Oh, you never know, I'm sure she has spies everywhere," I couldn't help but suppose.

He laughed. Turning around, he hung up some suits in the changing stall. "You know what I've never done? A movie montage. Hot actresses always get montages of themselves, with their friends, trying on outfits and stuff."

Standing to one side of the rack, I gave him an incredulous look. "I don't think Connell Rhodes has many opportunities to try on clothes in the dark world of Rouin. But hey, maybe if you suggest it, they could do it as a fan service."

"Yeah." His eyes lit up, piling on to my joke. "Who knows? There could be some rundown mall in that post-apocalyptic universe and he just can't decide which distressed leather jacket he should wear to most effectively fight off bad guys." He held up two suits against his tall frame, one after the other. "What do you think?"

Pursing my lips in realization, I tilted my head, giving him a look of mock disbelief. "Are you trying to do a montage right now?"

He laughed again. "Why not?" He hung the suits back up. "My stylist already pre-selected all this anyway, so they should look good."

I was sure they would all look *phenomenal* on Brandon's freaking perfect build, but that was beside the point. "Would you just please pick one so we can get going?"

Half-rolling his eyes, Brandon shrugged off his sports coat and tossed it onto the couch. "You're no fun." As if he'd forgotten I was there, he started to unbutton his shirt. But he paused on his second button to glance up at me. His eyebrows rose in a devilishly mischievous inviting look. "Care to assist me?"

I almost turned liquid right then and there. Forcing an incredulous scoff, I gave him a hard nudge backward into the dressing booth and closed the door. "Cut it out. We're going to be late."

Brandon burst out laughing again, his laughter muffled by the door now separating us. "I was just kidding, Rye."

I squeezed my eyes shut for a moment. Was I actually preferring for Brandon to return to his cranky, stoic version right now? For sure, I wouldn't be this nervous if he did. It was absolutely not fair that someone so annoyingly, unbelievably arrogant had to be so annoyingly, unbelievably hot—and charming, and funny, and generous.

I had to wring my hands out to calm down the shivers again. It was already taking all of my willpower for the images of Brandon from that underwear photoshoot not to come rushing back into my mind. And now he was changing clothes in that stall a mere few feet away.

Just tonight. Keep it together for tonight, Rye.

Shaking my head, I plunked myself down on the couch to check my phone again. But I couldn't make myself sit still. Standing up, I wandered around the gallery myself. Balmain's also had a gorgeous selection of clothing for women.

My eyes almost popped out of my head when I turned over the price tag of a bohemian flowered top. Definitely way out of my price range.

Brandon emerged from the booth adjusting the neck of a beige linen suit. Even with my back turned, I almost caught my breath at his reflection in the mirror. "Too fancy?" he asked.

I turned to meet his gaze. The light coloring of the suit complemented his sandy blond hair, glimmering under the tiny spotlights on the ceiling. He almost glowed in his hotness. "No, it's... it's..." I had forgotten how to form words. Until today, I would have never said *any* beige suit looked good on any man. But damnnnnn... "Yeah, good..." I trailed off with a shrug.

A small smirk hung around the corner of his mouth as he watched me fluster. "I know, right? Irresistible."

Shaking my head again, I buried my face in one hand—half in exasperation, half to cover my face turning red. "Did you say 'incredibly arrogant'? Then yes."

Brandon chuckled. He didn't sound the least bit offended.

I forced my attention down to my phone to check the agenda calendar, or at least to ground myself back to reality. "It looks like you've got a shoot tomorrow morning. After a Late Late Show taping." My eyebrows furrowed in question. "Why would you schedule an interview right in the middle of a busy shoot?"

Brandon's expression turned dull. "Clearly, we thought we'd be done by now."

"Oh, hey," I piped up with another idea—mostly to distract myself. "You should post a social media update right now. What do you want to say?"

"I couldn't care less."

"Come on," I urged. "You could say 'Last minute shopping for an outfit for Late Night' or something." I was already typing something and Brandon craned his neck to look over as I swiped, typed, and switched screens around.

"You follow me?" He sounded surprised to see the status.

"Of course I do."

"Hey! What the hell is this?" His tone easily shifted into shock as he snatched the phone from my hand for a closer look. *Somehow*, he had glimpsed my GPS tracking app. He shot me a sort of scandalized wide-eyed look. "You freaking lo-jacked me!"

"Oh!" I jumped in alert and tried to get my phone back. "No—I mean, yes, but um—"

The look he gave me seemed more astonished than upset. "Oh my god. That's how you found me at that fortune teller hut in Silver Lake or that tiny café in the Arts District. I should have known. Nobody is that clever."

Grabbing my phone back, I couldn't help my self-satisfied grin. "Well, clever enough to lo-jack your phone."

His jaw dropped, even though he still only seemed highly amused. "I think I should press charges. That's a huge invasion of my privacy."

I sucked in a breath, almost in panic. "You wouldn't dare."

Brandon laughed out loud. "No." He met my gaze, a halfway lazy smile on his face. "I don't know what it is. I kind of like you keeping tabs on me."

"It's my job, isn't it?" I quipped, matter-of-factly.

He blinked, the light in his eyes fading a bit. "That's right." He seemed stunned for a moment.

My eyebrows furrowed in concern. I was about to ask if his injury was paining him, but he cleared his throat and turned back to the rack of suits to select another one.

"Um, so," he started again, "how's it going with Ian?"

"Ian?" I echoed in puzzlement.

His voice had a layer of ambiguity in it. "I thought you wanted to ask him out. Or maybe that Steve guy."

I almost scoffed in mocking. "Sure, let me just clear my calendar and pursue a personal life, shall I? I don't know if you noticed but I only have time for one needy male in my life right now. And fortunately for you, that position is already currently occupied."

Brandon barely stifled his grin. "Well, I'm honored." He cleared his throat again. "You mentioned something about an ex-boyfriend before," he asked offhand. "He sounded like a jerk. You're not still hung up on him, are you?"

I shot him a narrow-eyed look.

"What?" He shrugged innocently. "You already know everything about me. I can't ask about you?"

I sighed, not really eager to rehash the story. "Let's just say when he met me...well, that girl was a mousy, little nerd whose main skill set seemed to be multi-tasking." Rueful, I pursed my lips. "Couldn't really blame him though. He wouldn't have ever anticipated that down the road, some-how, she'd turn into some kind of flighty artist. So there went that four-year relationship."

He huffed. "What an idiot."

I couldn't help an amused chuckle. "I'm...so glad you ap-prove?"

His hands paused on the suit rack as if he was mulling something over. "I never slept with my other PAs," he de-clared out of the blue.

"What?" I blinked, a little taken aback by his extreme change in conversation topic.

I thought Brandon's cheeks almost colored. "I mean, at least I don't make that a habit. Just in case that's what you thought."

Frowning, I averted my gaze to try to recall. "But every-one said—"

Taking another suit with him into the dressing booth, he poked his head out for a moment. "Seriously, Rye? You al-ready know you shouldn't believe everything you hear," he chided before closing the door behind him once more.

17

Chapter 17 - Late Late Night

When we arrived at the Late Late Show studios, I was relieved to relegate myself to the shadows.

I enjoyed watching everyone hustle and bustle around Brandon. Everyone seemed super thrilled to have him there, and Brandon was friendly and engaging. It was such a refreshing change from past shoots when I'd often had to repeatedly apologize to everyone for my client's rudeness and brash behavior.

But Brandon strode on to that stage to resounding applause and cheers like the happiest guy in the world. He sat on the couch and spoke animatedly about his past movies, this current season of the show everyone had been working so hard on. He even responded to questions about his "small" accident on set today with grace and tact.

For some weird reason, I felt proud of him.

Not that I felt I could personally claim responsibility for any of his successes, but just for today, I felt that I had performed my job to the utmost, got my client here on time, and in good spirits, no less. I supposed that was as much as any PA could claim.

The host ended the segment with a karaoke sing-along and I almost couldn't believe it when Brandon actually took up that microphone with confidence to croon along.

Looking out at the audience, I couldn't help my awe at everyone's response. Brandon's voice was so velvety smooth and rich, I was sure every female in that audience instantly fell in love with him—if not all over again.

Suffice it to say, Brandon charmed everyone, and in that dark gray suit with a tie as deep blue as his eyes, he looked as hot as humanly possible.

Irresistible indeed...

After the show, when Brandon stepped off the stage, I was waiting behind the red curtains.

His smile widened when he met my gaze as he strode toward me.

I feigned clapping as I beamed at him. "You were so great. I—" Before I knew what was happening, he picked me up to whirl me around. I gasped in surprise, automatically holding on to his shoulders. His sturdy frame beneath me, those strong hands braced against my hips instantly made me tingle all over as the world whirled around me.

A chuckle rumbled in his chest. He set me back down, the smile not leaving his face, his eyes never leaving mine as he towered over me, his arms loose around my waist.

A bit breathless, I gave him a questioning look. "What was that for?"

He looked like he wanted to say something else, but he just shrugged and took a step back. "You're a good cheer-leader."

I almost swayed off-balance at the sudden absence of his warmth.

Was I drunk?

I didn't have any of that champagne at the boutique. We only had root beer in the limo.

I wanted to step closer to Brandon again.

He was still standing in front of me as if he'd forgotten what he was supposed to do next. Like if I asked, he actually would take me in his arms again.

I sucked in a breath and took another step back. "Um, I guess you should get changed." I gestured toward the hallway leading to the dressing rooms.

Brandon still didn't move. Those stormy blue eyes darted around hesitantly before meeting mine again. He opened his mouth to say something but—

"Rye," one of the show's assistants tapped on my shoulder. "I sent through that marketing material you approved for Mr. Fyfe's publicity reels."

I nodded, somehow still unable to look away from Brandon just yet. "Thanks, Colleen."

"Oh, and Mr. Stewart wants to confirm the dates for Mr. Fyfe's junket schedule. It's for updating the website. Could you quickly check it?" She beckoned me over. "It's at my desk."

I took a deep breath and turned to give Colleen a small smile. "Sure. I'll take a look." Without another glance back at Brandon, I turned to follow Colleen to the back office.

"Come on, Annie," I mumbled to the ringing against my ear.

Annie hadn't been picking up her calls since she'd texted that they'd all gone out to dinner after the game, and I seriously needed someone to talk me down this metaphorical ledge I felt like I was about to jump off.

"Annie!" I yelled at her message service. "Did you catch the show? Why aren't you picking up? You all better be okay right now, you hear me? Also, you need to tell me what to do—give me another distraction. Where are you guys going to be in half an hour? Maybe I can meet up with you. Is Steve still around?"

I stalked down the hall toward the dressing rooms to get my stuff so we could leave. Brandon was probably already waiting at reception. I was told Lou was already coming around with the limo.

My nerves were shot. I couldn't stop thinking about Brandon, that dazzling, charming smile, how incredible it had felt to be in his arms, what it might feel like to have those arms around me again, or wanting to hang out in the limo and even just watch TV with him again—all day tomorrow maybe.

I shouldn't think about him this way. I was sure I had so many reservations. What were they again? Right then, I couldn't remember a single one.

I stared at the scribbled name on the star on the dressing room door yet again.

Brandon Fyfe.

"I had to watch him try on clothes today, Annie," I hissed in frustration. "Do you understand what I'm telling you right now? I'm not nearly equipped enough to deal with this next level of hotness. At one point, Brandon tried on this cotton V-neck button-down and I was this close to swooning. I swear to god if I see it again, I'm going to ruin that damn shirt and tear it off him with my teeth," I declared as I pushed through the door.

Stopping short, I gasped when my gaze fell on Brandon's tall form across the dimly lit room.

Oh, shoot. He was still here!

Brandon turned around. But the way his eyes were wide indicated more than surprise. It indicated, among other things, that he had heard *everything.*

Putting my phone away, I stammered in absolute panic. "H-hi. Sorry, I-I didn't know anyone was in here—I mean, you—that you were still in here."

After a pause, one corner of his mouth turned up. "It's fine. Don't worry about it."

My mouth went dry.

Brandon was just so tall and lean. He had taken off his suit jacket and was wearing that damn soft cotton button-down V-neck, with the sleeves rolled up to his elbows, highlighting those toned forearms.

He took a step toward me.

I backed up. "Um, were you getting changed? I think I—I should uh..." I couldn't tear my gaze from his throat, his broad shoulders.

"Maybe you should come closer," he suggested, his voice almost a low husky rumble as he took another step. "I mean, if you need to tear anything off with your teeth, I'd want to make it easy on you."

My stomach did a nosedive, but I didn't know if I wanted to cringe in embarrassment or shiver with eager anticipation. "I'm fine. I-I'm really—I'm really—" When I stepped back again, I had my back to the door.

Brandon tilted his head to regard me with a look. "You *were* referring to this shirt?" He reached up to undo the top button, exposing more of that toned, tanned chest.

My heart was pounding hard, I almost thought I was going to faint. But there was nowhere for me to go and when he took yet another step, he was close enough that I could feel how warm he was. My gaze was still locked on his shirt-front as he undid yet another button.

Peering at my face, he dropped his hand. "Care to assist me?"

Swallowing hard, I dared to look up to meet his challenging gaze.

In spite of myself, I wanted to wipe the self-assured smirk off that handsome face, the highly amused sparkle in his eyes.

He'd already heard what I'd said. I couldn't pretend I hadn't said it. I couldn't take it back. It was too late now.

I couldn't run away.

I didn't want to run away.

Letting out a slow exhale, I lifted shaky hands to slip another button undone on his shirt. Suddenly emboldened, I ran my thumb against the soft fabric before accidentally-on-purpose slipping my hand underneath it to play over his hard torso.

That made him groan in his throat.

I couldn't help a gratified smile at his reaction. His skin felt hot under my hand even as I almost involuntarily slid my palm up his bare chest.

Closing his eyes, Brandon groaned again. He gave the belt loops of my jeans a rough tug to pull me toward him until my body was flush against his. "Christ, Rye. You're making this really hard."

My pulse raced at the sudden realization. He wasn't rejecting me. He wasn't stepping back. He wasn't running away either.

He wanted this.

He wanted this too.

When those mesmerizing deep blue eyes gazed down at me again, I couldn't help staring up into them. His expression was raw, open, as if inviting me to peer into his soul, beyond all the façades and pretenses.

And I saw him.

I saw his pure molten desire, his glowing confidence...but there was still also a little hint of uncertainty in his eyes. That little bit of insecurity as if he wasn't sure he deserved all of this, any of this. Even with all his talent, all his charm, his incredible spirit—even if he genuinely deserved everything—there was still that fear in him that his dreams may just be that too far away.

That if he really asked for what he wanted, he would be told 'no'.

I felt a twinge of resolution spark inside me as I gazed up at him.

I wanted to be his 'yes'.

Brandon lifted his hand to brush against my cheek. "I wish I knew what was going on in your head right now."

Self-conscious at the intensity of my thoughts, I was sure I flushed scarlet. "Oh, you really don't."

"Are you thinking about me?" His eyes narrowed but the almost-desperate hope was evident on his face.

I bit my lip. "Maybe..."

His grip on my chin tightened as red-hot want flashed in his eyes. His gaze zeroing in on my mouth, his next question was gravel rough. "Are you thinking about my mouth too?"

I was already heaving against him. It was easy to lie, but less easy to disguise my heart pounding in my chest. I opened my mouth to answer but he spoke first.

"I'm thinking I want to put my mouth on yours. Right now." With his thumb, he stroked my lower lip, his voice rougher and lower with intensity and need. "I've been thinking about it for weeks." He moved slowly, angling his head as he leaned closer. "I'm thinking I'm going to like it. Very, very much."

I shivered as he pressed me back against the door. Unable, unwilling to move away, despite that little nagging voice in the back of my mind, telling me to hesitate, trying to regain its hold on sense and reality.

The moment his lips touched mine, I let go.

And Brandon held nothing back, his warm lips kissing me so hard, my insides melted in instant surrender.

His kiss was electrifying. I felt it everywhere.

Closing my eyes, I slid my hands up his strong chest to curl around his neck, my fingers digging into that soft, thick hair. With a pleasured grunt, he slid his arms around my waist to crush me closer against his form.

I kissed him back almost as desperately as he was kissing me, as though he couldn't get enough of me. His hands were in my hair, on my back, then even lower... Unable to help myself, I shoved the half-buttoned shirt off his chest and shoulders, running my fingers across his hard torso, those arms, sculpting every inch, every muscle.

He groaned so loud in his throat it was almost a growl and he deepened the kiss further. His tongue slid into my mouth as if he couldn't help himself either. He tasted like an explosion of root beer and mints and I wanted more.

I wanted it all.

I broke off kissing for a moment and he chased my lips for a second, letting out a sound of displeasure, but before he could voice a complaint, I dragged my lips across the base of his throat, his collarbone, his bare chest, and the next sound he made was tugged from deep within him.

"Oh my god, Rye. You're going to kill me."

His fingers wrapped in my hair, giving it a hard tug, so he could swoop down and take my lips again, more roughly this time, more desperate, slanting his mouth against mine, immersing himself in our kiss, in us.

Brandon pulled away, heady and breathless. He met my gaze with his intoxicated, heavy-lidded ones, his voice barely a whisper as he spoke only two words.

"My place?"

<h1 style="text-align:center">18</h1>

Chapter 18 - Morning After

Something was tickling my ear when I woke up.

Still groggy, I squinted at the sunlight filtering in through the drapes hanging on unfamiliar windows... in the unfamiliar room—an airy space with a minimalist aesthetic, probably matching the rest of the penthouse.

I'd never had to drop by his apartment before, even for errands, but I easily recognized the designer décor from when it was featured on MTV.

Almost with a gasp, my eyes popped open as it struck me exactly where I was. Or more accurately, whose bed I was in. But I didn't move.

Well, I couldn't.

Brandon's arm was slung across my shoulders. His warmth was all down the length of my bare back as he cradled me against him. His large hand was propped on the fluffy down pillow in front of my face. My own fingers looked tiny and delicate entwined in his.

My heart thundered in my chest as I remembered everything that happened last night.

Brandon was absolutely incredible.

Even with everything that I knew about his reputation, I still had clearly underestimated him. And somehow, he was intense and gentle at the same time. I definitely didn't expect how enjoyable that would be.

This was all very, very, definitely unexpected.

I frowned when my gaze fell on the red numbers of the digital clock on the bedside table.

7:46 a.m.

"Oh my god." I jerked in bed, even though I still couldn't sit up.

That woke Brandon though.

Still sounding half-asleep, his lips grazed my shoulder with a murmur, "Good morning."

Shivers ran up and down my entire body once again. My stomach did a flip as the full impact of what had happened was slowly registering in my brain. "I have to get up. Brandon, I have to go." I shoved his arm off so I could twist away and straighten up, almost tweaking my ankle.

Hissing under my breath, I grabbed my clothes off the floor to put them on in a hurry. I paused for a second to glance backward—which was something I really should've thought the better of.

The sight of Brandon all gorgeous and adorably rumpled in bed, shirtless, the navy sheets tangled around his bottom half, boxers low on his hips, tugged at my stomach again.

He must have noticed the look on my face. His eyebrows rose in an expectant prompt, a sly smirk on that irresistible mouth. "See something you like?"

That's beside the point! I almost yelled out, but I settled to letting out a groan of frustration as I hopped around, trying to get my jeans back on.

By the coffee table, I stared at the blank screens on my work phone, *and* Brandon's, *and* my personal phone that were all haphazardly strewn there.

I gaped back at Brandon again when it hit me. "You turned off all the phones? When?"

Most of last night was a blur. When did he even have a chance to do that? How did he even have enough presence of mind to think to do that?

Shifting in bed, he shrugged. "When you were in the bathroom, you know. Before."

"Oh, no." Panic nearly seizing me, I grabbed all the phones. The moment I turned them back on, the room was filled with a cacophony of ring tones, beeps, and alerts. "Oh, crap."

I grabbed his phone again first for a semi-frantic scroll through some apps. "Do you think anyone saw us last night? Saw me? Oh god." I closed my eyes for a moment in dread. "Do I even want to check what hashtag is trending on social media right now?"

"Relax. Nobody saw," he assured, his tone vaguely confident. "I made sure of it. We left the Late Show through the delivery bay and came in here using the back entrance."

I smacked my palm on my forehead. "What about Lou? Ooohh, does he know I'm here?"

"No." Brandon ran his fingers through his hair. He seemed unusually subdued as he simply watched me flutter around in my chaos. "Lou went back to *Lightscape* after the show. I told him you met up with some friends in the city and that I was going to stay the night here."

My eyes bulged, half in disbelief. How did he already plan for everything already? How often did he do this?

My gaze darted around restlessly trying to organize my scattered thoughts. What else did we need to check? Did we need to bribe any security guards who might have seen us? Was my day going to be full of calls to make up a story to cover this up?

What in the hell was I even thinking last night? In the light of day, every tiny ramification flooded every cell in my being. Every reservation I somehow couldn't summon last night was suddenly very, very present in my mind, front and center, with flashing red lights.

Dismissing all the questions in my foggy head, I focused on getting dressed so I could leave as quickly as possible. Frowning, I picked up my shirt from yesterday and my face flushed hot again. I hadn't even noticed that Brandon had ripped off some buttons last night from...um, the urgency.

Shaking it off, I cleared my throat. "Could I borrow a shirt or something? I seriously can't show up on set looking like this."

He gestured carelessly toward a box near the door. "There's a bunch of souvenir shirts over there."

I walked over to the box. Lifting up a shirt to examine it, I made a face. It was one of those merchandise t-shirts from the show. "This has your big head on the front."

Brandon glanced up with a small grin. "Yeah. Doesn't it look great? It's for my fans."

"I am not wearing this."

Leaning back against the headboard, he looked way too pleased with himself. "Suit yourself. Show up on set wearing your 'walk of shame' clothes." He folded his arms across his still bare chest, with a self-satisfied, arrogant grin.

I rolled my eyes in resignation. I reached into the shirt to turn it inside out before putting it on, the big printed face on my back.

Brandon's grin faded. "Oh, come on." He got up to walk across the room, easily reaching for the hem of the shirt to tug it up and off of me once again.

"Hey!"

He leaned over to steal a quick kiss—I jumped in my startle—before he grinned again. "Fine. You got me." He gestured to one of the shopping bags on an armchair. "Look in there."

Shooting him a still-suspicious look, I moved to peer into the bag.

My jaw almost dropped in surprise as I lifted the flow-ered bohemian top from Balmain's I'd been looking at last night. I met his gaze again but I was too stunned, I couldn't even say anything.

He flopped back into bed, his smile widening again. "I knew that would come in handy."

I couldn't help shaking my head. "You are too good at this." I quickly put the top on and tied up my hair in a messy ponytail. "Look, they need you at the studio in fifteen min-utes. You'd better be there." Checking my watch, I blew out a breath. "They needed me at the studio two hours ago. Crap."

"Don't worry about it," he dismissed with a wave. "Tell them you're sick."

I tilted my head in consideration. "Oh, I must be. Either that or I'm pretty close."

I had to dodge the pillow he threw at my head. In two more seconds, I was out the door.

19

Chapter 19 - Like Normal

I was never more paranoid in my entire life than I was when I sneaked out of Brandon's building. But I was sure I would look even more suspicious if I hunched over and tried to slither away. So I put my shoulders back and hurried out of there, trying to make it seem as though it was just another day, and that I was just on another urgent errand from my client.

My super famous, super hot actor client—who absolutely rocked my world last night.

Although, I couldn't quite figure out if I was the new notch on his bedpost or if he was mine.

Before my brain exploded with overwhelming thoughts, I decided to push the whole thing out of my mind for the moment.

When I arrived at the office, it was business as usual at *Lightscape* studios.

I only had to field one or two questions about why I was late. That was, I told everyone it was because I had a hang-over—because I'd 'met up with my friends for drinks' (Note to self: Remember to make sure to tell Annie too in case she needed to cover for me) after the Late Show taping. A concept everyone seemed to automatically understand.

But at least nobody yelled at me for being late.

Then again, since Brandon had also come in late, it wasn't like I'd held anything up myself.

By the time lunch rolled around, I chewed on my lip as I read Annie's text message 22 of 36.

HELLO? WHY aren't you answering?????

The rest of her messages from last night were in the same vein—asking where I was and what had happened. But this felt like something I should tell her about in person. I decided it was better to wait until I got home.

Apparently, Steve had just gone home after dinner, and Annie and Enrique had gotten...busy, which was why she hadn't answered my calls.

If I wasn't already freaking out, I would have found that endlessly amusing.

When I arrived at the catering tent, one of the production assistants, Maureen, gave me a warm smile. "Fyfe looked happy today. Congratulations on last night."

I froze like a stunned possum. "What do you mean?"

Her eyebrows rose. "The Late Late Show interview? He did great!"

My knees weakening in relief, I almost collapsed. "Oh. Yes. Of course." I kept the smile on my face until she walked away, resisting the urge to bury my face in my hands.

Way to look even more suspicious, Rye.

I'd been elbow-deep in sorting files in the office when I was told Brandon had arrived and headed straight to shooting all morning—which was fortunate.

I wasn't sure I was prepared to face him again quite so soon.

Oh, jeez. I would still have to see him every day.

Every damn day of this damn job.

I scolded myself yet again for my inability to hold it together. I had just put my dream job entirely at risk.

My mind swirled with worst-case scenarios and what-ifs.

If Debra found out, my job would be over.

If the paparazzi found out, my *life* would be over.

Calm down, Rye.

I shook my head to clear it.

It was one night.

It would never happen again.

Things could go back to normal now.

I selected a bagel from the basket and loaded it onto the conveyor toaster, content to stare at the machine as it moved along while I attempted to reset my brain.

Back to normal...

Everything was going to be—

I felt his warm presence behind me before the words whispered near my ear.

"I can't stop thinking about your mouth."

My face flushed instantly but I caught myself before I squeaked.

Count on Brandon Fyfe to say the exact wrong (right?) thing at a time like this to make everything from last night come screaming back to me. My every nerve stood up on end, but I seriously couldn't tell if it was from anxiety or excitement.

Clearing my throat in a half-futile attempt to compose myself, I gave him a sideways nonchalant glance. "Um. Hi."

Brandon's grin was suggestive. "I haven't seen you all day."

I moved along the table. "Yeah...um, busy."

His voice was still low as he followed behind me. "You left so fast, we didn't get to talk. Plus...I wanted to kiss you again."

A delicious shiver shot up my chest at the rumble in his tone.

Oh, dear god.

I had to look up and around to make sure everyone else was well out of earshot. My heart pounded in my chest. This was so not the place.

But Brandon it seemed, couldn't take the hint. He went on, "So, last night was fun."

"Mm-hm." I placed my toasted bagel on a paper plate, almost gritting my teeth. I had to get him to stop talking. If anyone even remotely suspected anything, I would be as toasted as this bagel.

Walking to a table with my plate, I resisted the urge to smack my forehead. What had I even been thinking?

Sleeping with Hollywood's 'Most Likely to Devastate Your Heart', the 'Hottest Blond Hero of the Year', People's Magazine's 'Sexiest Man Alive'?

I couldn't even blame him. I totally did this to myself. I'd wanted to get with this infamous playboy of a celebrity and now he'd gotten some of this.

Frowning, I stopped to think.

Wait a minute.

He'd *already* hit this. So what was Brandon even still doing chasing me up again?

I would have figured—in fact, I would have fully expected Brandon to be hitting up the next hot actress/intern on the staff now that he'd got his current PA into bed.

There was a burst of laughter from across the tent, and even though it highly likely had nothing to do with me, I still felt suddenly queasy. A couple of girls near the salad bar cast a curious look and I dropped my gaze.

Familiar nagging voices droned on in my head.

Is this what you left your real career for? To sleep around with some actor?

A light flashed at the end of the table and I nearly jumped. Some of the other staff were just taking photos of the catered food with their phones, but my hands felt clammy, my skin felt cold.

Did Brandon think that I was the kind of girl who would sleep around to get ahead in this job?

Was he expecting that I would be happy to offer it again whenever he wanted now?

A sinking feeling in my stomach almost bowled me over.

Oh god.

Brandon noticed that I almost dropped my plate. He peered at my face. "Rye?"

Whirling around to meet his gaze, I sucked in a breath. "Mr. Fyfe—"

Brandon gaped at me, echoing in ridicule, "*Mr. Fyfe?*"

Trying to stay determined, I pursed my lips. "Look, Mr. Fyfe. I'm sorry if I've given you the wrong impression. Last night—that—wasn't a service I was providing." Keeping my voice low, I shook my head. "It's not part of my job as your PA. If you're expecting that I would do any of that again whenever you want, I'm—I'm—deeply, deeply—"

His eyebrows snapped together at my fluster. "Stop." He took my plate to set it down on a table before taking my arm. Before I could protest, he led me around the catering tables near the back of the tent then let me go. "Take your phone out."

I almost winced at his brusque instruction. "What?"

"Just do it."

I took my phone out of my pocket to show him. "Why...?"

He tilted his head. "So it doesn't look suspicious that we're talking like this." His forehead creased with concern. "Rye. Breathe." I almost thought he was going to reach for me—it looked like he wanted to—but he only clasped his hands together.

His chin set in determination. "First of all, I would never expect that sort of service from you—or anyone—as part of this job. Secondly, I'm sorry. Maybe I should have waited until we were alone to talk to you about it, but..." He dropped his gaze. "I've been busy shooting all morning and when I saw you here, I—guess I just couldn't help it." Glancing over my shoulder at someone passing by, he raised his voice a little, "And reschedule that appointment for next week."

I kept my focus on my phone. I supposed it was a relief at least to know that he understood the need to keep this looking as work-related as it could be, and sincere or not, his reassurance had soothed my panicked, racing pulse.

When I looked up at him again, there was a solemn imploring in those eyes, a hint of uncertainty in that small smile. But when I looked away and let out a sigh, his smile faded altogether.

"Oh, I get it." He nodded. "This is the part when you say last night was a huge mistake and that we shouldn't do that again."

I swallowed, taking a beat to construct my response. "No." I shook my head to disagree. "No, it wasn't a mistake."

Brandon raised his eyebrows in skepticism.

"But we definitely shouldn't do that again," I concluded, turning to exit the catering tent altogether. I wasn't feeling very hungry anymore.

He trailed behind me. "Well, that's just poor logic," he reasoned, the overt self-confidence back in his tone. "Obviously, given those conditions, we should definitely do that again, once or twice—*a day* maybe." He leaned closer. "And I still want to kiss you," he spoke under his breath. "What time does the shoot finish?"

I let out another helpless sigh. "You do understand we shouldn't do this, right? I mean, last night was..." *Mindblow-*

ing. Phenomenal. Exceptional. "—nice, but...we would both get in so much trouble if anyone found out. Me more than you, most likely."

Indignant protest was all over his expression. "Nice?" he echoed again. "Rye—" he tried to argue.

Stopping to face him, I shook my head with my firm declaration. "No! That's it. You can't. I can't. We can't." My chest squeezing in remorse, I spun to walk away even faster. But I didn't have to.

Brandon stopped in the middle of the lot, as though I had punched him in the gut again.

Maybe I punched us both in the gut.

20

Chapter 20 - Developments

"Wake up, Rye!"

I felt like Annie was yelling in my ear.

Groaning in complaint, I rolled over in bed, eyes still shut. "Whaaat?" I was still groggy from getting barely four hours of sleep in from working late last night.

"Wake the hell up and look at this!"

Oh wait, Annie *was* yelling in my ear.

My nose caught the fragrant flowery scent before I opened my eyes. My blurred vision focused on what looked like a hundred red roses in a fancy bunch shoved near my face. "What the hell...?"

Annie plopped the giant bouquet on the coffee table as I moved to sit up. Folding her arms across her chest as she stood beside the couch, she gave me an expectant look. "Care to explain?"

"Explain what? Enrique gave you flowers, congratulations," I mumbled, rubbing my eyes.

"Um, no." She shook her head. "The courier said they were for Miss Rye Williams." Then her eyebrow rose. "But there's no card. So who's it from?"

"What?" I still couldn't wrap my head around what was happening.

Dropping to her knees to peer at my face, Annie shot me an eager-to-get-excited look. "Oh my gosh, girl, are you finally dating someone?"

I looked from Annie's wild, excited eyes to the humongous bouquet of flowers, back to Annie, and back to the flowers. They were so beautiful—the fresh, scarlet red roses with the smattering of baby's breaths. Was it really a hundred roses? I swallowed hard. Nobody had ever before given me anything so...so...freaking expensive!

"Hey!" Annie shook my shoulder. "What actually happened to you the other night? After getting all of your messages, I was half-panicked when you didn't come home."

Finally standing up, I let out a sigh. "I'm sorry! *I* was panicked when *you* weren't replying to me." I went to the bathroom to wash up with Annie trailing behind me.

She gave me a lopsided grin. "Sorry about that. I almost forgot to give you the good news." She thumped on my shoulder. "Enrique and I are finally moving in together! That's why we were um...busy celebrating."

My jaw almost dropped with my toothbrush still in my mouth. "What? That's wonderful!" I moved to hug her but she pushed me away.

"Ew, don't drip toothpaste on me!"

I chuckled through a mouthful of foam. "Fine, I'll hug you later. Congratulations."

Annie gave me a hundred-megawatt grin. "Thanks." Her tone turned huffy. "If you ask me, it's about bloody well time." Then her face flushed again with a giggle, I almost laughed myself. She looked so happy.

"Well, I'm very happy for you guys," I bid as I finished up in the bathroom.

Annie went on, "I'll probably be moving into his one-bedroom apartment across town. So another bit of good news. If you're happy to stay here, I can sublet it to you."

My eyes widened. "Ooh wow, that's a pretty big move, Annie." Almost flustered as my brain went on overdrive again, I picked up my phone to check some messages. "I mean, I'll need to double check a few things, if I can afford it and stuff, and if it makes sense, but if you can let me know in advance how much—"

"Wait, wait, wait." She put her hand up. "Before I even forget, let's get back to the elephant of roses in the room." Her eyes went wide as dinner plates once again. "Where exactly did you spend the other night?"

I made a face. "Well, I was going to tell you yesterday, except you came home later than I did. Something happened after the Late Late show."

"Something...?" she echoed. "Something good?"

I nodded but I also cringed further. "With Brandon."

Annie's eyes nearly popped out of her face. "Oh my god, are you okay?"

"Yes," I replied quickly in case she thought otherwise. "Fine." But I couldn't help my cheeks flushing warm again. "It was...it was...*really good.*"

Her jaw had dropped so low, I almost had to scoop it off the floor.

It seemed my revelation had rendered her completely speechless. When she still didn't say anything more for about a minute, I waved my hand in her face. "Yoohoo, Annie! Are you still alive in there?"

Annie's gaze slid to one side in a wistful fantasy. "Sorry, I was just imagining it. Whew!" She fanned herself.

"Annie!" I tossed a pillow in her face. "Enrique would be shocked."

She burst out laughing. "Please, it's not like he doesn't know what crazy shenanigans go on in my imagination already. Besides, I was the one who told you to do your boss and get it over with. I suppose congrats to you are in order as well."

"Somehow, I'm not so sure about that," I mused as I picked out what to wear. "I mean technically he's not really my boss. But I've just potentially jeopardized my career, pathetic as it is. And you *know* what my folks would say."

Annie rolled her eyes. "Who cares what your parents—or anyone else thinks? You're a responsible adult. You're now responsible for ruining your own life if you want."

Groaning, I closed my eyes for a moment. "Thanks, Annie. Very supportive."

"Hey, at least, you got it out of your system," Annie rationalized, heading to the kitchen to make her morning smoothie. "Just think of it as a hurdle you've overcome. And now you can get back to work." Humming happily to herself, she collected her usual odd collection of fruits and vegetables to throw in the blender. "Right?"

Still deep in thought, I snapped to attention so I could respond to her. "Right." I couldn't help my frown as I mulled over her words. Taking a deep breath, I nodded anyway, "Right...back to work."

I was sitting under the tent in the studio lot later that morning, begrudgingly wading through boxes of freshly delivered merchandise with my trusty clipboard, because of course I still had work to do.

At least, you got it out of your system. Just think of it as a hurdle you've overcome. And now you can get back to work.

I held on to Annie's words like a mantra.

Logically, I knew sleeping with my client was the highest level of impropriety, notwithstanding Debra's zero-tolerance uber strict policy on dating in the workplace. I really shouldn't have even done that—that much was clear.

But that was the whole point of everything, right?

It was a wonderful once-in-a-lifetime experience.

Curiosity satisfied.

I just meant do him. Have it all done. Get it all out of your system.

Only I felt like I hadn't even accomplished what Annie's advice had set out to do.

God help me, Brandon Fyfe was even less out of my system than before.

I didn't want to admit it but...I wanted more.

I stared at the catalog of novelty can coolers with snapshots of Connell Rhodes from the show spread out on the table before me. In each one, Brandon was, of course, looking all broody and hot and sexy as hell, with that mussed-up hair falling across his forehead, those lips, those hands...

Unbidden, an odd shiver shot up my spine.

It was already virtually impossible to get through the most mundane of my daily tasks without remembering how it had felt to be with Brandon the other night.

He was just so good at...*everything*.

Holy crap. How was I even supposed to move on from this? I'd probably never date again. Brandon had just set a peg so impossibly high, no other guy was probably ever going to be able to compare.

Faint squeals and screams broke into the usual busy hum as the door to the *Lightscape* meeting room swung open.

I easily caught Brandon's gaze from across the lot as soon as he stepped out.

They'd been holding private 'Meet and Greet' events for Brandon's super fans today, and about a dozen or so fans followed him out of the room post-session with some last-minute opportunities to interact in person with Connell Rhodes, ask all the questions under the sun, and get every piece of paraphernalia from the show (or the occasional body part) signed.

There wasn't really much controlling the thrilled super fans, except for the presence of a couple of security personnel to make sure nobody got too handsy.

Of course, Brandon, true to form, soaked up all the attention.

Except while he was signing notebooks and taking selfies, he glanced up to lock eyes with me another few times.

Like a crazy person.

Like someone purposefully inviting suspicion and gossip into his already highly easily scandalized life.

And even at that distance, with the hint of that perfect smile hanging around his lips and that knowing, almost wistful look whenever he met mine, I almost couldn't help the warm flush on my face.

Being an actor, I was sure he could mask a whole range of emotions, but after where we left things yesterday, I expected a certain degree of coldness, of wariness. But Brandon didn't look fazed or upset at all. In fact, somehow, those intense eyes only looked even more determined.

I wasn't sure if that was a good thing or not.

Shaking it off, I put on my most nonchalant face and straightened up to walk over.

Work. I still have to work.

Armed with my sample catalog and clipboard, I approached the squealing mass of bodies around the man of the hour. I fidgeted in my stance, ready to wait for as long as required. I caught Brandon's glance again for a split second before averting my gaze.

Brandon cleared his throat. Putting his hands up, he gave the crowd a little bow. "That's all for now, please. Thank you all so much for watching the show."

I almost jumped in surprise when he grabbed my elbow and whirled around to lead me away. When he was sure we were out of earshot, Brandon slowed his pace. "Sorry that took so long."

"No, no." I shook my head. "You didn't have to rush off. They were all so excited to see you."

"I know." He cracked a small smile, dropping his gaze almost diffidently. "But I was more excited to see you."

21

Chapter 21 - Bad Ideas

Brandon stretched out on the couch in his trailer, lazily playing with his sunglasses, not saying anything. He seemed content to just watch me rattle off the items from the to-do list on my phone.

"You need to approve the new merch that just shipped in," I recited. "Lauren is still waiting on that list of gala invites. Davis wants an update on that audition you missed the other day—quote 'annoyed, stop turning them down'—end quote. And the P.T. wanted to schedule your follow-up—what? What?" Putting my phone down, I stopped to prompt, raising my eyebrows in expectation. "Why are you looking at me like that?"

A self-satisfied smirk graced that gorgeous mouth. "You're not mad at me anymore."

I let out a sigh. "I was never mad at you," I corrected. "I just wanted things to be clear, you know, between us. This is just work. We need to keep things professional."

"Why?" He gave me that patented devilishly charming smile of his. "You afraid you're going to fall madly in love with me?"

At the overconfident look on this face, I couldn't help my burst of laughter.

Brandon's smile faded. He feigned an offended look. "It's not that funny," he mumbled. "Maybe I want you to."

"Oh, I get it now." I nodded as if I just had an epiphany. "I see why all your former PAs quit. You slept together then you immediately proposed marriage and sent them running for the hills. *That's* what happened." I smacked my palm on my forehead. "How did nobody else figure this out?"

He narrowed his eyes. "Be careful what you wish for."

"Mr. Fyfe, you are out of your mind." I was determined to keep a level head. "You don't have to patronize me. We're both mature enough to call what happened that night what it was—a one-night stand. Now can we please just get back to work?"

"No." Brandon stood up with a grimace. "How can you be so rational about this? Look, Rye." Fidgeting on his feet, his eyes darted around, almost seeming at a loss for words. "I—really like you."

That almost stopped me breathing. I resisted the urge to pinch myself to check if I was daydreaming, but the twinge in my chest felt very, very real.

I repeated his words in my mind, the way he'd said it, the look in his eyes, the husky timbre in his voice, I wanted to capture it, save it.

Some actors were good at acting in real life too—pretending, lying. Even if Brandon was doing both, right now, it really felt like neither. I wanted it to be neither. Even if there was nothing we could do about it.

He ran his fingers through his hair. "Also...I had a really good time the other night."

I let out a slow breath. I could at least resign to that fact. "I know. Me too."

The confused crease on his forehead deepened. "Then why can't we do it again?"

"Look," I began, matter-of-factly, "I've given it a lot of thought."

"So did I—"

I whacked his arm to wipe that mischievous look off his face. "Not that kind of thought," I chided. "And I gotta tell you, I had no trouble convincing myself that it would be a bad idea."

He puffed out his chest. "Try to convince me then."

"Alright." I licked my lips before ticking off items from my fingers. "First of all, you're an actor so that means dating you is out of the question. Secondly, I'm your PA and I think that it would just be totally distracting, not to mention unprofessional. Lastly, I would get into so much trouble. You know Debra has a zero-tolerance policy about this and I really need this job."

Brandon was watching intently as I spoke. "Your mouth makes excellent points." He leaned over to kiss me before I could say anything else.

"Watch it!" I jumped in alert. "Someone could walk in." Grabbing his arm, I pulled him toward the back room and shut the door behind us. I double-checked that the curtains were drawn and made sure there were no other production staff hanging around the rear of the trailer just in case.

But Brandon, in all self-assuredness, turned to me with another devilishly handsome, mischievous grin. "Why Miss Williams, you've just led me into a room with a bed. Was that on purpose?"

"No, dummy. It's just it'll be easier for us to talk in here with nobody accidentally bursting in."

Stepping closer, he backed me up against the door, caging me in with his body. "It's also easier to kiss you in here." His face hovered close to mine, but he didn't lean in. He seemed content just holding me close, studying my face.

"Brandon," I began in exasperation.

Except it must have sounded like a breathy sigh, he took that as a cue to bend his head to nuzzle the side of my neck, his lips near my ear. "Mm... My name sounds so good when you say it. I want to listen to you say my name all day long, all night long..."

A pleasurable shiver shot up my spine at his words, his warmth, his touch.

Oh, this is such a bad idea...

I closed my eyes anyway.

My heart pounded in my chest. Was this the stuff of dreams? It was supposed to be simple. I liked a guy and he liked me back.

But I knew nothing would ever be simple with 'Hollywood's A-listers'. I knew enough about other celebrity scandals for sure. I already almost was one just the other week, with what was nothing but an innocent café meeting over hot chocolate.

We probably wouldn't be able to do any normal things, like a regular date at a regular restaurant, with wine, chocolates, flowers...

My eyes flew open as it struck me just then. I had to stop my jaw from dropping. The flowers. That must have been why he figured I wasn't mad at him anymore. "Wait. *You* sent the flowers."

Straightening up, Brandon blinked. "No. What flowers?" His forehead creased. "Someone sent you flowers?"

I frowned in confusion. "It wasn't you?"

"No."

I narrowed my eyes at him in suspicion, then tilted my head to venture again, "Oh, right, so it *wasn't* you."

"No, it definitely wasn't me." He shook his head with a little mocking scoff. "Why would I send you flowers?"

"Right." I nodded slowly. "Sorry, my mistake." I took a deep breath. "I guess Ian sent them to me."

Brandon froze. "What?"

Looking away, I shrugged. "It must have been Ian. He sent me this really gorgeous bouquet of two dozen red roses to thank me for dinner the other night," I fibbed with a smile. "I mean, he already did send flowers before our date. I guess he's just that generous to send another one afterward as well."

Brandon's throat tightened visibly.

"You know what, I should send him a 'thank you' note—" I pushed away to rummage in the shelf for a pen, reaching for a post-it from the bedside table.

"Fine!" Brandon threw up his hands. "You win." He shook his head, looking mostly annoyed with himself. "I sent them. The flowers were from me. And for your information, there were a hundred red roses, if you even bothered to count them."

Highly amused, I half-stifled my chuckle. "How did you even order flowers? Did you finally figure out how to make outgoing calls on your phone?"

He shot me a suffering look. "I asked Jillian for a favor."

I jerked up straight in near panic. "Jillian knows about us? I mean, about this?"

"No," Brandon answered quickly. "Look, she knows I sent some flowers to an address. Unless she's snooped around in your employee file to find out where you live, I don't think she'll figure it out quite so quickly."

"Oh."

"Did...you like them?"

The look on his face was so tentative and unsure, it almost made my heart melt. I couldn't help the warm flush in my cheeks. But before I got all carried away, I cracked a smirk instead. "I thought you said you weren't the sending-flowers kind of guy. Also, you suck at playing chicken."

"It's not funny." He tugged me closer again to ask, short of growling, "Tell me you didn't really go out with Ian."

The almost desperate look in his eyes surprised me. "I didn't. I really didn't." I tilted my head. "Are you jealous right now? We're not even actually together."

Already shaking his head in disbelief at himself, he cradled my face in his hands. "You already know, I'm not usually like this."

I studied those intense blue eyes but I knew he was right. I'd never seen him like this before. Not counting several episodes of the show, certainly not in real life over the past several weeks.

Lifting my hand, I brushed that wavy hair aside off his forehead. My stomach stirred at the notion that I could be this close to him. That out of all the rich, classy, beautiful actresses he was surrounded with every day, he wanted to be with me, to touch me, to kiss me. The mere notion of it was already intoxicating.

I knew it was still a bad idea but...

Brandon groaned low when my fingers grazed his ear. His gaze dropped to my mouth and I willingly tipped my chin up.

A loud knocking on the door startled me enough to shove him clear across the room.

"Mr. Fyfe, it's time for your next 'Meet and Greet'," Jillian's calling out was muffled from the front end of the trailer.

Making a face, Brandon let out a groan of annoyance. He straightened up and headed for the door. "Hey, Rye, block out some time on my schedule later tonight."

My heart was still pounding in near panic. Reeling in my nerves, I nodded quickly. The context switch caught me somewhat off-guard. It appeared I was his PA once again. "Okay. For what?"

"I want to have dinner with you."

22

Chapter 22 - Jealous Much

I chewed on my fingernails.

"Good morning, Rye!" Victor waved at me under my usual tent from across the lot. It looked like he was headed into *Stage 31*.

"Hey, Victor." I gave him a wave back before returning to chewing on my fingernails.

I was supposed to be sorting merchandise and packing three dozen PR boxes. I was supposed to be focusing on work and not thinking about Brandon. I was supposed to have outgrown this fingernail-chewing habit like ten years ago. But today, I was doing none of that.

I wasn't even sure if I was relieved or disappointed that Brandon had to last-minute cancel our dinner plans last night.

Had I taken great pains to get ready and looked forward to dinner for a change? Sure.

Did I make sure I wasn't going to eat pizza or fried chicken in front of Brandon while he had to eat his carb-free platter? Of course.

Did I understand that a reshoot was the most high-priority thing ever in a delayed production? Absolutely.

Oh well... that fancy dress and those high-heels had been under my office desk for a few days. It was probably good timing that I managed to bring them back when I went home last night, alone, with my box of salad.

There had been no avoiding telling Annie either. It turned out I wouldn't really make a very good actress since my dour mood was apparently all over my face. Except Annie didn't quite understand what the problem was.

"Didn't you say it yourself? Big, high-profile actors don't go out with regular people," she reminded me. "I do get it, you know. This feels super exciting. But maybe if you really think about it, instead of being disappointed, you should be relieved to get this reality check."

Trust Annie and her logic formulas.

I'd even said it myself. This couldn't really happen. It made so much more sense to keep my distance and not stir the pot.

It was better. At least this way, I didn't have to keep hanging on to false hopes and be strung along—by a famous celebrity no less—who was likely to be attracted by the next shiny Hollywood object that sashayed along and eventually drop me like yesterday's tabloid news.

Maybe Brandon already figured too that the moment had passed. He realized he'd merely been hit by a bolt of crazy the other night, and now that he'd gotten some sense knocked back into him, he was over it.

We would both have some closure and move on.

On the upside, I couldn't stop hearing about Brandon's surprisingly inexplicable motivation and enthusiasm for the work from everyone. And with the star of the show so focused, it made everyone else up their game too. I'd never seen production roll quite as smoothly as it had for the last week or so.

Admittedly, on that score, I was very happy for him.

"Rye, come here!"

I jumped up, automatically grabbing my phone and a box of mints.

Brandon was fast-walking toward *Stage 31*. I'd almost gotten used to the sight of him smiling, that the frown on his face looked almost dangerous.

We stopped by his chair beside the set, dressed as another dark alley today. The staff were still working on some of the props and adjusting backdrops and lights around.

Peering at his face, I held out the box of mints. "Are you okay?"

The look he gave me was almost tortured. "Look, about dinner—"

I was already shaking my head to dismiss his apology—absolutely unwilling to open up that can of worms.

"Hey, Brandon!" one of the recurring character actors from the production walked up to us from across the room. "How's it going, man?"

Patrick O'Callaghan, dark-haired and beefy, was the second love interest, because, of course, there must always be some type of 'love triangle' in these types of shows.

He turned his honey-brown gaze to me with a smile. "And I don't think we've met?" He held out his hand. "My name's Patrick. I'm the other monster hunter in the show."

Taking his hand, I smiled back. "I'm Rye. I'm sort of Brandon's PA—really, Lauren's PA, borrowed from Debra." I shook my head. "It's a bit complicated."

"You sound like a woman of many talents," Patrick remarked. "I'm sorry to say my only other field of expertise is football. I used to play in college, but now I only play for fun."

"Oh, that's right. I think I remember reading about that. You got Defensive Player of the Year a few times. That's amazing!" I couldn't help but gush.

Brandon's eyebrows furrowed instantly. "Alright, alright, it's nice to meet you too." He moved to pull my hand out of Patrick's grasp to take it firmly in his. His warm fingers enclosed mine as he tugged me along. "Let's go, Rye."

"Alright, people." Walking onto the set, Maureen, the production assistant seemed already wearied in her announcement. "It seems Miss Sinclair is running a bit late. Again." She glanced up at me, near the back. "Oh, hey, wait. I have an idea. Rye, come here." She beckoned me to come over.

I blinked in surprise. "Me?"

"Come stand over here." Not patient enough to wait, Maureen came to take me by the shoulders and veered me toward the set, with Brandon inadvertently dragged along behind me.

"We just need to get this blocking in before the shoot," Maureen explained, eyeing the top of my head. "Yeah...you're almost the same height as Betsy." Then she waved Patrick over. "Mr. O'Callaghan, let's do one run-through of this scene with you and Rye."

Still holding onto my hand, Brandon jerked in his stance. "What?" He glanced from me to Patrick and back to me again. His eyebrows still furrowed in displeasure.

"Mr. Fyfe, we don't need you for this shot." Maureen motioned him back.

I shot Brandon a pointed look, shaking my hand so he would let go.

Still with that glower on his face, Brandon dropped my hand and slowly stepped back, but only as far as his chair by the sidelines.

Patrick gave me a sunny smile as he approached. "Hello again." He leaned over to whisper. "Don't worry if you're nervous. Blocking is really easy. I usually just pretend I'm one of the props and get moved around."

That made me laugh. "Thanks, I appreciate the advice."

The director ran us through the scene quite a few times, instructing me and Patrick where to stand, adjusting every so often to make sure they could get what they wanted in the frame, while someone drew chalk marks on the floor.

"Okay," the director went on, "next, Betsy, you've just been shot by a poisoned arrow and are about to die—"

"Again," Patrick quipped with a wink at me and we both laughed. It was almost comical the number of times the writers killed or almost killed Betsy in the show.

"...and Merrick comes to save you," the director went on. "We're doing another Season 1 Episode 13."

My eyes lit up. Long-time fans of the show would forever remember that episode as the day the fan ship *Metsy* (or *Betrick*) was born.

Accordingly, I knelt on the floor and Patrick took his position crouching in front of me.

It was just a blocking check. The set was super noisy. Everyone was bustling around with a purpose. There was no theme music playing in the background. It wasn't anywhere close to being realistic.

And I knew Patrick was absolutely not actually going to kiss me. So I wasn't sure why I was suddenly still all nervous about it.

I watched Patrick's face as the director yelled out instructions behind us to fix whatever was on the set to get in the shot.

Patrick's dark hair complemented those bright hazel eyes. He could probably cut pudding on that sharp jawline, even with that amiable smile on his friendly face. His shoulders, seemingly broader than Brandon's, were clad in an expensive brown leather jacket.

Then it struck me.

He was downright gorgeous too, but...I *didn't* want to kiss him.

The director clapping out loud snapped me out of my reverie. "Alright, guys," he called out, already pulling out his phone to check messages or something.

Straightening up, Patrick held out a hand to help me stand. "Good job, Rye."

"Thanks, Patrick."

"Rye!" Brandon snapped from the sidelines.

I almost groaned. I could probably count on my one hand the days when Brandon didn't bark my name in impatience. "What?" I trudged off the set and behind the cameras where he was.

Like an irate hawk, Brandon watched Patrick heading toward the other end of the set before leaning over to me. His next instruction was spoken low, almost under his breath. "Go back to the office right now."

I shot him a ridiculous look. "Why? Are you worried the director's going to make me stand next to Patrick again?" I suggested, fully in jest.

Brandon's jaw visibly clenched.

"You can't be jealous right now," I mocked in a hiss, reminding him yet again. "I told you we're not even together."

Brandon's warning rumbled from his chest. "Don't start with me, Rye. So help me, I'll push you up against that fake alley wall and kiss you in front of everyone—so hard you'll forget your own name."

My breath caught in my throat, my gaze dropped involuntarily to his mouth.

Dammit.

What the hell was wrong with me? Even after everything I had already resolved in my mind, I still almost actually wanted him to do it.

I spun on my heel and exited stage left before I did anything else I already knew I was absolutely not supposed to do.

I shouldn't like Brandon.

Except I still did.

I should be counting my lucky stars right now that a guy I liked actually liked me back.

And he was so sweet and witty—and so incredibly, freaking hot.

Ugh. Groaning, I buried my head in one hand, while the other tapped absently on my keyboard as I worked to purge a virus from some of the office computers after 'someone' (Read: Shawn) allegedly accidentally downloaded something nefarious from an email attachment.

If only the consequences weren't so catastrophic if Brandon and I actually did start going out. It would be a total disaster. If only we'd met at literally any other time or place, or under completely different circumstances, maybe there might even be a chance for us.

But it was definitely not here and now.

It seemed I still needed to make Brandon understand this.

I needed to explain how we really couldn't go any further and how utter nonsense it was for him to be getting all possessive and jealous.

Although, I was almost ashamed to admit that making Brandon Fyfe jealous felt a teensy bit thrilling. It certainly wasn't something every girl could say.

"Rye, oh good, you're here." Lauren popped her head into the *Lightscape* offices. "I need you to do something for me."

I looked up. "Sure. What do you need?"

She motioned a camera clicking with her hand. "Go to the set and take a couple of behind-the-scenes snaps of the coordination after the scene they're shooting for the publicity reels. I heard Rhiannon Sinclair finally arrived, so get some shots of her too."

Gathering my stuff together, I nodded as I got up. "Gotcha."

Rhiannon Sinclair was the actress who played Betsy on the show. I hadn't met her yet but I'd read her bio already, much as I'd read everyone else's on the production's cast list. I'd read that she and Brandon had (of course) dated for a while during the first season and that she hated doing stunts.

Hopefully, I wasn't about to take a publicity photo of her looking horrible attempting a stunt scene.

Taking down some last-minute notes using the stylus on my phone, I sneaked into *Stage 31* as quietly as I could to make sure I didn't disturb the shoot. Except I very nearly tripped on my own feet at the sight of the scene they were in the middle of shooting.

It was time for the *Betnell* shippers to swoon.

Betsy and Connell were making out in the exact same alley set as before.

The scene was lit, the set was quiet, and the fake fog was blowing in as Brandon took Rhiannon in his arms and covered her mouth with his. Again and again.

Swallowing hard, I glanced at the camera guys and the production people in the dimly lit space beside me, as if I needed some form of confirmation that it wasn't real.

Twirling the stylus between my fingers, I watched from behind the camera. But as they shot and reshot the scene, there was a sinking feeling in my stomach that wouldn't go away.

For god's sake, Rye. You said it yourself. You are not together. It's stupid to be jealous.

Brandon's fingers were in Rhiannon's hair, touching her face, her mouth...

I was so tense, I very nearly snapped my precious stylus in two, but I couldn't seem to look away. It wasn't the first love scene of Brandon's I'd seen from his shows. I mean every woman in the world was always so crazy jealous of Betsy every time these types of episodes aired. I just never figured that at some point I would also be one of them.

When the director yelled "Cut! Thanks, everyone." I couldn't help my sigh of relief.

Thank god.

Maureen walked on to speak to Brandon and Rhiannon for a few minutes.

Shoot! I snapped to attention, pulling up my phone to take some photos of the three of them talking amidst the un-lit set.

I'd almost forgotten to do my damn job.

Ugh. This was exactly why I shouldn't be mooning over my freaking client. Didn't I even tell him this already? It was totally distracting!

Fortunately, I got the shots I needed before Brandon gave them a nod for whatever reason, seemingly ending the conversation. "—do that later, sure," he was saying over his shoulder as he walked off, passing by me toward the *Stage 31* doors.

Wordless, I held out his water bottle and pack of mints and followed behind him.

He took a big gulp, pausing to glance back at me. He swallowed before he spoke. "What?"

"What? Nothing."

He frowned at my uncharacteristically subdued response. Then eyes wide in realization, he paused in mid-stride. "Wait." He gestured to the set behind him. "That didn't bother you, did it?"

I looked away. "No. Not at all. It's your job, isn't it? You get paid to make out with hot actresses all the time. Over and over and over..." I couldn't keep the revulsion out of my tone as I brushed past him.

Following me, Brandon cracked a highly pleased smile. "Oh my god, you are so jealous right now." He gave me a pointed look. "Didn't you just say we weren't allowed to be jealous because we weren't actually together?"

Making a face, I was fully prepared to deny it.

He glanced up and down the lot before leading me around the back of the sound stage building.

Stopping, he gave me a pout, reaching up to cup my cheek in his hand. "Baby, Rhiannon kisses like a pleco catfish. That's part of why we broke up years ago. If they didn't pay me, I wouldn't kiss her."

In spite of myself, the oddly specific metaphor made me chuckle.

Dropping his hand, Brandon shook his head. "It's acting. It's not real." He frowned again as if realizing something else. "I might have to do a bit more of this in the show. It's my job."

Unable to help a slight frown, I still nodded. "I know." I guessed I'd already realized that, but I didn't guess that it would bother me this much.

His expression turned serious for a second as he gazed down at me. "Do you trust me?"

I looked deep into those blue eyes, but I could only tell him the truth. "I-I don't know yet."

Brandon clenched his jaw as though my words stung him, but he was undeterred. "Trust this." He pushed me back, his body pinning me against the wall as his mouth came crashing down on mine—just like he'd said he was going to do in the alley set earlier.

He kissed me so hard, my lips would surely be swollen afterward.

I clutched at the front of his shirt to keep him close. Like if he let go, I would disintegrate and float off into the ether.

Aimless. Joyless.

Forgetting to care altogether, I melted in his arms.

I wanted to stay with him, spend all day with him, even if all we did was watch hockey games on TV. I wanted to be his cheerleader. I wanted to always see that charming smile, wanted to be the cause of it, wanted to take care of him, make him happy every day.

I wanted to be the only one he kissed like this.

I wanted him to be my 'yes' too.

Even if it ruined me.

Oh my god, I was falling for him.

I was falling for Brandon.

Brandon Fyfe.

Voices coming closer made me jump in alarm.

Brandon broke off to meet my gaze, his eyes still glazed.

"No, I'm sure he's—" Coming around the corner, Ian stopped short, his eyes nearly popping right out of his head as his gaze fell on the two of us in the secluded spot behind the building.

Crap! My face burning, I tried to pull away but Brandon seemed to have other ideas. He held me fast to keep me against him, before giving Ian a silent, pointed, meaningful look.

Possibly noting Brandon's glare and my too-obviously-recently-kissed lips, Ian stifled an amused chuckle. Slowly shaking his head, he called back over his shoulder, "Never mind. I think I saw Brandon go to his trailer. Why don't you guys go check over there?"

Looking back at the two of us with a smirk, Ian was still shaking his head, but he didn't say anything else. Turning on his heel, he simply walked away.

Squeezing my eyes shut, I buried my face in Brandon's chest. "Oh, god."

Chuckling, he stroked my hair. "Don't worry about Ian," he assured. "He won't tell anyone."

I shot him an annoyed, but still mocking look. "Sure, 'cause you inspire such loyalty in your friends."

With an exasperated half-groan, half-chuckle like he couldn't figure what to do with me, Brandon buried his face in my neck, nuzzling softly as his strong arms folded around me, pressing me warm and tight against him, nearly lifting me off my feet. "You smell so good," he murmured. "Feel so good... I want to take you home right now." He pulled away for a moment. "We're finished shooting for the night. I can get someone to bring my car around so we don't have to get Lou to drive."

I gave him a playful shove away, almost in disbelief. "Oh, you've really got everything all sorted, don't you? I knew it from the last time. You *are* too good at this!" I threw up my hands. "I mean, you had everything prepared after the Late Late Show taping. Seriously, how often do you sneak women up to your downtown loft?"

He grimaced, seeming almost hurt by that. "It's not that I do that sort of thing often. It's just that... that night, I wanted it to be perfect." Shrugging, he met my gaze with a small smile. "I wanted it to be perfect for you."

And my heart did a little flip.

Oh, danger...
Goddammit, *he* was perfect.

23

Chapter 23 - Real Stuff

When I wrenched my eyes open, I almost had a heart attack when I realized I was pressed against Brandon's bare chest, his arms warm and secure around me.

An easy chuckle rumbled from him. He was already awake.

I squinted up to look at him—his handsome face almost freaking glowed in the daylight. "What?" I croaked.

Brandon's smile widened. "Your heartbeat got really fast and I knew you were awake."

Mortified, I closed my eyes. "Oh god." Almost in a panic, I sat up with a start again. "Oh god, wait—" He loosened his hold on me enough so I could reach over and grab my phone from the nightstand.

My eyebrows furrowed in confusion. I checked the other phones. "Huh."

"Everything okay?"

I glanced back at him for a moment, my focus still on the phones.

No new messages.

"That's weird," I couldn't help but comment.

Stretching to sit up himself, Brandon took a deep breath. "What's weird?"

"I don't...have any messages, or calls, or anything." I shifted back to show him all three phones.

He slung his arm around my shoulders again to tug me closer. "Isn't that good?" he murmured against my ear before nuzzling my neck.

"No. I'm sort of afraid the world may have ended."

I felt the self-confident grin against my bare shoulder. "I suppose I could understand why you might be of that opinion after last night."

I coughed out an amused chuckle. "No. Look at this. It's past seven. I should have *some* messages from the studio at least, surely."

Brandon studied the concerned look on my face. "Don't worry, Rye," he assured. "I took care of it."

Pausing, my eyes widened a bit. "Took care of what...?"

He cracked another grin. "I...sort of told everyone to push everything back two hours today. And...I sort of told them not to disturb me—or you." Before I could start, he shook his head. "I didn't tell them why. I didn't tell them it had anything to do with you. I just said I wanted to get a bit of a later start today. Everyone was fine with it."

Still frowning, I studied his face. "Are you sure?"

He shifted like he was uncomfortable. "I didn't want you to rush off again like you couldn't wait to be rid of me, like you thought you'd made the biggest mistake of your life." With a small smile, he met my gaze again. "I thought we could have breakfast. I can make you coffee. I got bagels in the kitchen."

I shook my head again in disbelief. "You planned for this again."

He kissed my cheek. "I wanted this morning to be perfect too. As perfect as you are."

My heart squeezed.

I mean, he probably stole that line from the show or an audition or something. Still...nobody else knew that Brandon Fyfe was the sweetest freaking guy on the face of the planet.

I'd packed a spare change of clothes for myself so at least I didn't have to worry about my 'walk of shame' outfit. I didn't want to ask Brandon what that new shopping bag in the corner was for, in case he'd bought me more clothes. I didn't want to get any more overwhelmed than I was already feeling.

After breakfast and getting changed, I sat on the edge of the bed and began pulling out drawers from the nightstands to look inside.

Walking out of the bathroom, Brandon adjusted the cuffs on his sports jacket. "What are you looking for?"

"I thought I left my earrings here, you know, last time." I waved to dismiss my small issue. "I think I left them in a drawer to make sure they didn't get lost. I just forgot to get them when I left in the morning." I pulled open another drawer. "Aha."

With another one of those adorably lazy grins, he watched me put my earrings back on.

I furrowed my eyebrows. "Why are you smiling like that?"

Brandon shrugged. "Nothing. I...like that you leave things here."

I pursed my lips. "By accident. Not on purpose."

"Still," he quipped, looking entirely self-assured.

Amused myself, I rolled my eyes as I straightened up. "I can't believe you were jealous of Patrick O'Callaghan. I barely know the guy."

His smile fading, Brandon huffed. "He's always my number two. If I win an award, he's the runner-up. If I get 'top something', he'll get second place. On the show, he tries to steal Betsy all the time and now he's trying to steal you."

"He wasn't trying to steal me," I corrected with a scoff. "He stood *next* to me during blocking. Honestly, I wasn't even attracted to him."

The sun rose in his face once again. "Really?"

Chuckling, I made my way out of the room. "Hey, we should get a move on." I tapped the watch on my wrist. "We're about to be even later than you told everyone."

Brandon caught me from behind to tug me back in his arms. "Yes, ma'am," he murmured, even as he kissed the side of my neck, his nose in my hair. He groaned in his throat again. "Why do you have to always smell so good?"

Shivers running up my spine again, I tilted my head to one side to oblige him. The deep rumble in his chest hinted at wanting so very much more. I had to tamp down a bolt of fresh desire that shot right through me. He was going to make us even more late than we already were.

Still, it was *very* tempting...

The mere notion of Brandon Fyfe being my—ahem, boyfriend, was still almost too surreal to consider. But at some point, I was sure I would have to come down off of our little bubble here on Cloud 9 and deal with reality. And there really were so very many things to consider.

"I suppose we should tell Debra about this now."

He froze for a moment. "Um, yeah." He withdrew his arms from me. "Why don't you let me take care of that? I'll talk to Debra."

The vague evasiveness in his tone gave me pause. I gave him a sideways glance. "Well, we can both talk to Debra, right?"

For a moment, I thought a shadow crossed his face. But then he turned a bright smile at me again. "Of course. Sure. We can both tell her." He walked past me toward the lounge, my questioning gaze on his back, but he didn't say anything more.

"Okay..." Walking past the kitchen, my gaze happened upon the countertop. "What is this?" I picked up a manila folder. The title and author were clearly labeled across the front. "Why do you have a copy of my screenplay?"

Glancing back, Brandon shrugged. "I photocopied it 'cause I wanted to read it."

I blinked at him. "You photocopied something? By yourself?"

Seeming affronted, he gave me a pointed look. "Fine, I got someone to photocopy it."

Turning around, I clutched at my chest at my feigned offense. "You got someone *else* to photocopy something for you? Not me? I think I really should be jealous now."

Laughing again, he propped his chin in the crook of my neck to read over my shoulder as I flipped through the pages. "By the way, I really like this character 'Jack'—he seems pretty cool. It would be great though if he wasn't a total tough guy, right? If you ask me, most shows always just do these two-dimensional cliché characters."

Too amused to be offended, I gave him a sideways narrowed look. "Are you giving me critique?"

"Hey, from one pro to another, let's call it constructive criticism."

I was more than a little pleased that he was taking an interest in my stuff. I couldn't help a smile. "I like it."

"Besides, you give me critique all the time."

"Oh, is that whenever I tell you to stop being such a dumbass?"

"You can call me whatever you want, baby." He slipped his arms tight around me again. "Anyway, I told Nancy about my suggestions," he went on. "Like Jack probably needs something to soften his character—a favorite grandma or a pet. It would be so much better if he was more well-rounded, more real, you know?"

"What?" I stopped short.

"What?"

Pulling away, I turned to face him again. "You talked to Nancy about my screenplay?"

Brandon shrugged. "Sure, why not?"

My eyes popped wide. "Why? I didn't want to disturb her with my stupid screenplay."

His forehead creased. "But it's really good. Besides, if she says she likes it, then she might actually recommend it to the studio. And if *they* really like it, they might want to get you on board to actually make the show."

My skin tingling from an undefined anxiety, I cringed. "What's the point? It's not like I'm not busy enough running errands for you, and Lauren, and Debra."

"But you're a really good writer," Brandon pointed out. "Wouldn't that be a better job? There really isn't a career track for being a PA. I mean, you can't even get promoted."

A nerve ticked in the side of my neck from the suddenly familiar sentiments. "What...?" I had to stop my jaw from dropping.

"I mean, don't get me wrong." He waved his hands in front of him. "Being a PA is a good job. And you're really good at it. But what if you could get a better job writing? I already know you can do it. You could totally make it work."

Swallowing hard, I had to even out the tone of my response. I almost thought my hands were starting to shake.

"Everyone already thinks I've made a big mistake switching careers, Brandon. Please don't *you* start with me now too."

Grabbing my stuff, I spun to leave and headed for the elevators.

Brandon trailed behind me. "Are you getting upset?" he asked with a puzzled frown.

Pressing the button for the parking level, I settled back against the wall of the elevator across from him. "This is what I want to do," I reiterated as steadily as I could.

He tilted his head. "Running errands? You're basically living your life for someone else. I mean I understand it's a valid employment option for some people, but you—you're too good for this job. It's like you're..."

Staring at him in an impending rage, a keening noise screeched in my mind as he spoke the next words I almost already knew he was going to say.

"—wasting your talents."

It still hit me like a blow to the face.

"What did you just say?" I muttered through clenched teeth.

Brandon shrugged again, so very offhand. "I mean, I'm just wondering if this really makes you happy or if you're just scared to want more."

His tone was so authoritatively nonchalant, his expression so almost passive, I had to take a deep breath to make my counterargument.

"What about you?" I pointed out, tilting my chin up. "You already know you're not happy with your job right now, but you're not doing anything to change it."

Eyebrows snapping together, Brandon shot me a look. "What? What are you talking about?"

"You!" I threw my hands in his direction. "You keep going on and on about wanting to audition for other roles, but Davis says you've actually kept backing out of them. Is it because you've gotten complacent and too comfy with your position on this show? Or are you just afraid to try and fail too?"

He blinked like he was stunned, like I had hit precariously close to home.

I gave him a challenging glare. "You're too afraid to take a risk and change your life so you can be happy."

Brandon gave me a quick glance up and down. "Well...right back at ya!"

I didn't realize I was already heaving in upset.

His eyes were narrowed in confusion as he met my gaze. "Are we legit having a fight right now?"

24

Chapter 24 - The End

The car ride back to the studio was ominously quiet.

Brandon seemed as disoriented as I was about our little "fight" and had opted for tense silence—which was a relief. I hadn't been sure how to respond either, being that the nature of our argument was entirely new.

To a certain degree, it felt odd that he would be commenting on my life choices. Much as I expected it was weird for me to have criticized his work ethic all those weeks ago.

Back then, it hadn't been my place to tell him how to do his job. I was his PA, his employee.

But after last night, the dynamic change between us was more than a little unsettling.

I genuinely cared about him now. I wanted him to be happy. He probably said those things to me because he felt the same way. This was that line we never expected to cross.

I also couldn't shake the fact that, even if Brandon seemed to be singing the same tune as the rest of my family about my career change, maybe this time, he was right.

Was he right?

I supposed I hadn't really been planning further ahead when I set my sights on being the best PA in Hollywood. I'd just thought I'd level up somehow. But now that I was here, was this really enough for me? Or could there be more? Was I occupying myself with someone else's life only because I was scared to have my own goals?

Brandon dropped me off at the street corner before driving the car to the secured parking nearby so we wouldn't have to come in together.

If I wasn't already confused and upset, I would have noticed the just-as-ominous foreboding in the air as I arrived at the *Lightscape* offices.

Victor and Lauren were standing by my desk. The rest of the office was empty.

"Um...hi?" I ventured a greeting as I plopped my stuff down.

Lauren tilted her head to give me this look. "Debra's back from San Francisco."

"And she wants to see you in her office right away," Victor finished as though the two of them had rehearsed this.

Okay...

My heart pounded in my chest as I turned to fast-walk across the building. I kept swallowing to moisten my dry mouth.

This was it.

Trouble.

What the hell else could it possibly be?

Since, as someone had already so very recently eloquently pointed out, it wasn't like I should be expecting a promotion with this measly role or any such related good news.

Wide-eyed, I paused in mid-stride as I arrived at Debra's office's door just as Brandon was pulling it open. And even by the look on his face, my suspicions were easily confirmed.

Once we were both inside, Debra from behind her desk spun her laptop around. The browser had about a dozen tabs open but judging from the headline on the current tabloid website, they were all likely similarly themed.

Fyfe's mystery overnight guest's heated morning after.

The paparazzi had captured a snapshot of me and Brandon leaving his building not even an hour ago. It didn't look romantic, but the fight we were having certainly didn't make it look like I was simply there for an errand.

The article also had a collection of blurry photos of Brandon and me together—way too many. At the studio lot, on set, backstage at the Late Late Show.

Enough to cast that doubt.

Enough to make the front page—*pages*, plural.

All the blood drained from my face.

Yup. Trouble.

Debra's steely gaze was so heavy, I almost couldn't breathe. I dropped my gaze, wanting to disappear into a hole in the ground. I had zero defense.

Brandon opened his mouth as if to offer one.

"Don't even bother to deny it," Debra already cut him off, her tone sharp, cold, but equally wearied. "Brandon Fyfe, I told you once, I told you many times."

Brandon put his hands up. "Deb, this isn't what it looks like."

"And you—" Debra's no-nonsense eyes shifted to me.

Forcing myself to meet her gaze, I tried to speak despite the lump in my throat. "Miss Winger, I can explain—"

"You're fired."

Gasping in shock, my jaw dropped and I had to tamp down the wave of sudden nausea.

Brandon's eyes widened. "No, don't." He looked from me to Debra. "Look, it was all my fault. I was going to tell you. I thought you'd be back tomorrow."

Debra shook her head. "Brandon, I thought I was being very clear. Did you think I was kidding when I added that clause to your contract?"

Stunned, I stopped short. I thought I couldn't feel any more sick, but it seemed I was wrong. My heart dropped down to my hollowed stomach. "W-what clause...?"

Grimacing, Brandon's gaze dropped to the floor.

Debra folded her arms across her chest. "I explicitly said you were not to get involved with her, didn't I say that? Didn't I say there would be dire consequences?" She shook her head. "Dating is one thing. Sneaking around about it is quite another. All we have is our reputation. Maybe you two are good together, or in love or whatever, but that's neither here nor there. There are reasons why we have rules in place.

The fact of the matter is you've just made my job a little more difficult."

I had no response, no recourse. Debra was totally right.

"I almost thought that having Rye around was improving things with you, Brandon. You'd started coming to shoots on time and stopped antagonizing the staff. Then I come back today and I find out what?" Debra threw her hands up. "That you pushed back shooting? For her? For this? What do you think I'm running here? A dating service?"

My brain was still stuck on the other thing. "What clause?"

Debra tilted her chin up. "An additional two more years to his contract and his acceptance of this spring gig he'd been refusing to take on location for four months—*if* he got involved with you." She glared at me. "I guess I thought you were better than this, Rye. Or I would have written it into your contract as well."

I willed myself to be numb, if only to keep being able to breathe.

"Also what's this I heard about Brandon recommending your screenplay to Nancy? Is that why you're here, Rye? Is that why you took this job? Is that what you're using Brandon for?"

Bewildered and alarmed, I shot her a look, finding my voice again. "What? No!" Hot tears of mortification stung the edges of my eyes.

"No!" Brandon vigorously shook his head. "Rye would never do that." He met my stricken gaze. "I—I'm so sorry."

Debra rubbed the bridge of her nose. "Look, we are professionals. This impacts efficiency which impacts the bottom line. And you should already know how sensitive the climate is nowadays with these movements. As a female executive, it's absolutely vital that I ensure a safe working environment for everyone. Maybe it's too much, maybe I'm going overboard, but as you both well know, this is *my* business. And I will run it how I want."

I kept my gaze on the edge of the desk, my arms slack at my sides.

Narrowing her eyes, Debra took a deep long breath. "We're already behind schedule." She pointed her finger at me. "You, get out of my studio." She pointed at Brandon. "You—they need you on set right this goddamn moment."

Brandon shut the door to Debra's office as soon as we'd both stepped out.

I didn't even know where to start.

Although a strange calm was starting to come over me, if only as a confirmation.

This was exactly what I'd thought would happen.

When Brandon turned to face me, desperate imploring already in those blue eyes, I was almost already too exhausted to argue.

"You knew this would happen," I mumbled. "You knew *exactly* what would happen."

Unable to deny it, he grimaced. "Debra thought you were doing so well. She didn't want to lose you. She wanted to make sure I stayed away from you. She also knew I'd been wanting to get out of my current contract so..."

I blinked hard. "You made a deal. You made a deal about me."

The notion felt altogether reprehensible. Except I wasn't actually sure if I was upset about what he'd done or simply about the fact that he'd kept me in the dark about it.

"You should have told me. You *should*—" I added pointedly, "have kept it in your pants—but you should have also told me." I blew out another frustrated breath.

He seemed distressed. "I—I tried—I couldn't." He threw up his hands. "It's different with you. I've never had to try so hard not to be attracted to someone before. I didn't know it would go this far. And I was really careful to be discreet. Don't you think I already know the scandal if I was seen dating some lame, nobody PA—"

I shot him an almost offended look.

Brandon winced. "Crap, that's not what I meant." Closing his eyes for a moment, he set his jaw in resolution. "Those PAs before you... The truth is I made them quit."

"*You* made them quit?"

He let out a labored sigh. "I found one of them selling stuff stolen from me on eBay. Another one was some influencer, trying to boost her following by posting videos of me." He gave me a wan look. "It was pretty clear that they had only taken the job because they wanted their fifteen minutes of fame."

Rolling his eyes, he dismissed it with a wave. "Anyway, I'd had enough of their overt flirting, and they weren't too happy about me refusing their advances. It made them cranky and not good at their jobs. They had to go." He rubbed his face with his hand. "I was already so burned out by the show and all this. They were supposed to help me. They wanted to use me instead."

I shook my head slowly. The pained look on his face made me want to stroke his back to soothe him. "I'm so sorry, Brandon."

That almost made him smile. He studied my face for a long moment, as if he wanted to come closer, as if he wanted to touch me too, but he knew he couldn't.

"When all this started, I...thought maybe we could be friends." He shrugged, his tone muted. "I liked you. I liked that you were so good at your job. I liked that you didn't throw yourself at me at every opportunity." Pausing, he sighed. "I liked that...you treated me like I was just a normal person. If I was wrong, you would call me out. When I was being a jerk, you didn't hold back. And you definitely didn't pull any punches." Grimacing, he clutched at his stomach as though in the recollection.

I had to hide my chuckle in a cough. "I'm also sorry about that."

Brandon averted his gaze, a sort of quiet look in his eyes. "You encouraged me, pushed me. Even as a PA, you always went the extra mile for me." His chin set in resolution as he met my gaze again. "I shouldn't have made a deal with Debra about you. That was..."

"Heinous? Despicable?" I supplied, my eyebrows raised.

He put his hands up. "I knew Debra wouldn't offer me an out without something in return, so when she brought this up..." He gave a helpless shrug. "I guess I thought it was the only way."

My chest still felt hollow, but it wasn't like Brandon was the only one at fault. "I'm sorry too," I started. "I knew what we were doing. I knew exactly why we shouldn't have done it. I guess...you surprised me, and I... I liked you too." I rolled my eyes to add wryly, "Despite my best efforts."

Brandon almost chuckled. "I knew there was already that risk, but I liked you too much to not do anything about it. Honestly, I should have known it was already too late even the day we met."

I couldn't help a smile as I remembered that day in his trailer. If I was honest with myself too, I'd probably say the same thing. In retrospect, it was disturbingly clear. How on earth could I have possibly thought *I* could resist *him*?

Brandon held my gaze for another moment, as if he knew I'd realized the same thing, as if he wanted me to say it out loud as well, to hear it for himself, to confirm what we both already knew—

"Mr. Fyfe."

Brandon and I glanced over to see Lauren standing to one side of the office door, clipboard in her hand.

Lauren already had a slight cringe on her face. "We need you on the set now."

Of course.

Resisting the urge to shake my head, I dropped my gaze again and turned to go.

Brandon frowned. "Wait, Rye—" He caught my arm.

Sighing, I shrugged him off. "I need to leave now, Mr. Fyfe. I don't want to damage anyone's reputation any further."

Indignant protest was all over his face.

"Go. They need you," I urged, cracking a small smile. "Debra was right. You really can't afford to get distracted right now. You need to take all the time you can to finish this shoot." I took a deep breath. "And...I have to go find another job."

Brandon's forehead creased in deep concern. "That other shoot, on location, it's in Ireland. I leave right away. I won't see you again until I'm back in the spring."

"Then maybe it's a good thing." I tilted my head to regard him with a rational look. "Look, my life is so different from yours. Four months is a long time. If you find..." I trailed off with a resigned shrug. "I just mean, I don't want to wait for you so...don't even worry about it, okay?"

"Rye..."

I spun on my heel to walk across the *Lightscape* production lot for the last time, headed back to the offices so I could pack my stuff and leave.

Beyond the office building, in the warehouses, inside *Studio 31*, I knew everyone would still be tirelessly working on the show even after I'd left.

I knew Mickey, the press liaison, would be capable enough to be able to spin the story this morning and clean up the mess for Debra. The tabloids didn't have anything truly incriminating. The studio would be fine.

Brandon would be fine.
But me...
I was done.

25

Chapter 25 - The Beginning

I wasn't sure if I was packing up my desk or cleaning up the staff room. It seemed during my short tenure, I had accumulated quite a lot of Chinese takeaway containers and papers for upcycling. Most of what I was shoving off my desk was ending up in a giant black trash bag.

I leafed through a couple of article printouts and brochures with Brandon's annoyingly handsome face on it.

He'd gotten me fired.

Brandon Fyfe.

He literally screwed me in all the senses of the word.

So much for my dream job.

So much for my dream everything...

With a brisk shake of my head, I tossed the random paraphernalia into the trash.

"Hey, Rye." Victor came into the office, arms already held out to give me a hug. "Look, I'm not here to say goodbye, since I'm sure I'll still see you around town. You've got my number, right? So you know, whenever you feel like going out dancing or anything, you know who to call." He winked. "We do have those rare nights off, remember?"

I laughed. "I'll make a note of it. I mean, my calendar is suddenly wide open, if you get what I mean."

He clicked his tongue. "Nonsense. Clever girl like you, I'm sure you'll get snapped up by another job straight away. I know Lauren is still happy to give you a recommendation for whatever job opportunity you land next."

I scoffed. "Assuming Debra hasn't blacklisted me yet from all the other studios in Hollywood—or you know, California."

He thumped my back but curiously did not refute my statement. "You're going to be fine."

"So I guess everyone knows what happened? With me and Brandon?"

Victor wrinkled his nose. "If it makes you feel any better, nobody's blaming you," he offered, before amending, "—except maybe Debra. But I mean, honestly, everyone is pretty impressed with how long you held out against Fyfe's understandably debilitating allure and we all applaud you. Not Debra, of course."

I chuckled again at his continued need to qualify his statements.

He studied my expression. "Do you hate him?"

I wanted to smack myself in the face.

No. I didn't.

I didn't hate him. I just couldn't see him again.

Victor read the answer on my face and merely shook his head again. He looked around. "Has everyone come around to say goodbye to you yet?"

"Yup, Jillian and Shawn came through a few minutes ago. Lauren even passed on to me her lucky stapler." I held up the giant stapler covered in sparkly stickers. "I feel very honored."

Chuckling, Victor thumped on my back again.

I checked my watch. "Aaand I better scoot soon before Debra gets security to escort me from the premises."

Someone cleared their throat from the doorway.

When Victor and I looked over, I swear to god I almost fainted.

"Speak of the devil..." Victor mumbled under his breath so low, I almost didn't catch it.

Debra's intimidating presence was like a thousand days of rain on parades, with her chin up, her shoulders stiff. She was just such an impressive person. I knew she hated me but I guessed I still couldn't help but admire her.

Victor sprang away from me, passing by Debra as he sneaked away, his mumbles trailing off, "See you around, Rye. Hey Debra, good to see you. How was San Francisco? I love your hair. Did you change it recently or...?"

Eyeing the boxes around me, Debra took one step closer. "I'm not here to apologize."

I gave her a wan smile. "With all due respect, ma'am, I didn't think you were." I turned back to finish packing up my stuff. "I'll be out the door in a minute."

"Good." She gave me a curt nod. "You might think I'm the enemy, but I also just want to protect Brandon. Believe it or not, I actually care about him. I've seen him grow up—in front of the limelight no less, and you already know, that is no picnic for any kid. So if I'm a bit protective of him, that's why. I'd already made mistakes hiring his previous PAs."

I furrowed my eyebrows. "You know about his other PAs?"

"That they all had agendas? Yes. Brandon told me that day we amended his contract. I think it was the same day Tom Clooney was in the lot."

I blinked in realization. That would have accounted for Brandon's suddenly cranky disposition that day. Mustering up my courage, I lifted my chin to meet her gaze. I wanted to make at least one thing clear. "I'm not like his other PAs."

Debra merely tilted her head in consideration. "Maybe. Maybe you're different. Maybe you're the best PA ever. Maybe you'll make him the best girlfriend too, and stand by him through anything. But I don't know that," she finished with a firm shake of her head. "I *do* know Brandon. I know he's going to want to do anything for you, make sacrifices for you. He's going to move heaven and earth just for you. He's that kind of person." She took a deep breath. "And I can't allow that."

I wasn't sure if I was dejected or frustrated, or maybe I was still a bit intimidated by her, or maybe I'd already effectively numbed myself from the situation, but I couldn't access any rage. Maybe because I also understood exactly where she was coming from.

I nodded, subdued.

Debra moved to leave. Pausing for a second, she glanced over her shoulder. "I also read that script you sent Nancy."

Tossing another brochure into the trash bag, I let out a dull sigh. "And?"

"And you're definitely fired," she declared. "Because I think you're in the wrong job."

I whirled around, a stunned questioning look on my face.

But Debra was gone.

* * *

"Are you going to help me or not?" Annie grunted beneath the box of books in her arms.

It was moving day for Annie. Most of our cozy little apartment had been packed into various sizes of boxes. En- rique had been popping in and out all through the day to cart Annie's stuff into his car to drive across to his apart- ment on the other side of town.

Cross-legged on the couch, I was taking a break from emailing out resumes all across the city to look for another PA job. I'd been hyper-focused in my search for the past few days. No luck so far. No flat-out rejections or mob hit at- tempts either, so I was determined to stay optimistic.

I switched tabs on my laptop's screen. I'd been re-reading through my screenplay. I caught myself chuckling again from one of the lines I'd written. I supposed it was really difficult to view your own work as good. But encouraged by Brandon and Debra, I felt like maybe my writing really wasn't too bad.

Annie was puffing as she came back up the stairs to slump beside me on the couch. "Look," she began, "I know I've been pretty preoccupied with my stuff recently. Maybe I should have asked you more about how you felt, getting fired from that job."

I dismissed her with a wave. "I'll be fine. Don't worry about me."

She rolled her eyes. "I know you'll *be* fine. But you still haven't even told me if you wanted to sublet this apartment after I leave."

I glanced around the near-empty studio apartment. As it turned out, once Annie had gathered up her stuff, all of mine could still fit in one box. As if at any point, I was still expecting to up and move, to make sure I never stayed in one place. It seemed I hadn't committed to this life yet either.

"Annie, I think I need a job first before I can even think about where I can afford to live," I told her.

"What about moving in with your boyfriend?" she quipped.

I shot her a dagger look but she just burst out laughing.

"Ohh...too soon?" Annie slapped her thigh in mirth. She slung an arm around my shoulders. "Look, all that rumor chaos about you *allegedly* sleeping with Mr. Pretty Boy died down pretty quickly. I'm sure you could go see him again now if you wanted."

"Well, luckily, he's in Ireland now, so I don't have to risk the paparazzi hounding me again quite just yet." I shook my head. "Besides, you and I both know that little fling already had disaster written all over it from the get-go. It was never going to go anywhere."

Annie studied my face with a narrow-eyed look. I thought she was going to call me on my bluff—or this *lie* I told myself to make me feel better. Instead, she gave me a mischievous, prompting look. "Want me to give Steve a call?"

And we both burst out laughing.

My phone ringing broke through our dumb merriment and I went to answer the call. "Hello? Rye Williams speaking."

I sat up straight in alert as the woman calling said she was from another production studio and they had just received my resume. Giving Annie an eager look, I put my finger to my lips to motion her to shush. "Oh, thank you so much for calling."

"We'd love to get you in for an interview tomorrow. We think you're a good fit and you came highly—"

"Ooh is it a job? What is it?" Annie tugged on my arm. "*Where* is it? Near Sunset? Is it near Enrique's apartment?"

Furrowing my eyebrows, I strained to hear the woman on the phone. "Shut up, Annie!" I hissed, waving her away as I jumped up off the couch to take the call in the bathroom where Annie couldn't bug me.

I plugged my other ear with a finger. "I'm sorry. I didn't quite catch that. I was highly recommended by whom?"

And my jaw dropped to the South Pole.
Debra Winger, from *Lightscape* Studios.
That's what she said.
I blinked, stunned. "I-I was...?"

26

Chapter 26 - Written for You

Six months later

"How have you forgotten how to partition a hard drive already?" Annie made a face, tapping methodically on the keyboard on my laptop.

Sitting back in my chair, I sipped on my morning latte. "Sorry," I confessed. "I think that information already got pushed out of my brain by outlining strategies and plot structures. I'm telling you I've been learning so much these past few months."

With the weather turning warm, maybe Annie and I should have chosen to sit inside instead of outside the downtown LA café, but being that we didn't usually stay this long to meet up before work, it had totally slipped my mind.

"Are you going to be able to make dinner at our place tomorrow night?" She gave me a pointed look. "You know you've canceled on the last couple."

I made a face. "I'll have to let you know. Honestly, I've just been getting home and crashing in bed for the past few weeks. I won't exactly be good company." I sat up. "But, hey, my mom finally agreed to come visit me next month, so that's something."

Annie gave me an impressed approving look. "That's great!" She tilted her head in thought. "But can we invite her to my apartment instead?"

"What? Why?"

"Rye, I love you, but I'm still a little wary of that six-floor walk-up disaster you call an apartment."

I had to laugh. "You're such a snob. Just because Enrique's apartment has a doorman." Sticking my chin up, I huffed, "Besides, I like my apartment. It's cozy and it's right by tons of Chinese takeout places."

Her gaze returning to my laptop screen, Annie grinned somewhat wryly. "Congratulations on living the dream, my friend." She let out a big sigh, tapping a few more buttons before snapping the screen shut. "Okay, look, I've formatted the drive. But I want to install some drivers first later on, so don't use the partition yet."

"Gotcha, Miss Genius."

"Sweet." Not refuting my statement whatsoever, Annie drained her cup of coffee while checking her watch. "Miss

Genius needs to catch the bus to work now or Miss Genius is going to be late."

As we stood to leave, out of the corner of my eye, I noticed a couple of teens lingering by the door to the coffee shop. One of them was holding up her phone toward us, and when I glanced over, she sort of froze. Then tugging on her friend's arm, they both skittered away.

Tamping down the urge to roll my eyes, I merely shook my head.

Despite the fantastic clean-up job *Lightscape* Studios had done on my little blip of a scandal last year, there was no pulling those photos of Brandon Fyfe and me off the internet. So every once in a while, I would still get 'recognized' out in public. It wasn't official. Nobody knew my name. But there were enough blurred photos of me in those articles for people to suspect the resemblance.

Annie had noticed the onlookers' hasty retreat as well. She hooked her arm around mine as we walked to the bus stop. "Listen, I know I said I'd stop asking, but we both know you need to talk about this whole 'Brandon Fyfe' thing."

I gave her a confident look. "You know what, I actually think I've turned a corner. I've had a lot of time to think about what happened, and the past few months really helped me process everything."

I was proud to say I was no longer afraid to admit that Brandon Fyfe had been right about me. With the PA job, I'd been content to merely live adjacent to someone else's life, too scared of making decisions for myself. Not willing to deeply commit to any one thing. It had been partly the same reason my parents had been so worried about me.

"Seriously, Annie," I stressed. "I really think I've finally found my true passion, over, above, and beyond being a PA, especially now that I have this new job. I mean, what else do you think I'm afraid of?"

"Still afraid to be happy?" Annie quipped, matter-of-factly. "Didn't I hear Brandon Fyfe was already back from Ireland?"

"Oh, he's been back over a month or so," I relayed as nonchalantly as I could.

Annie shot me a wide-eyed look. "He hasn't tried to get in touch with you?"

"No. I mean, he doesn't have to," I pointed out. "I certainly don't expect him to."

She stopped to brace both hands on my arms and peered at my face. "It's just...you seemed to really like him. And then you seemed to give up awfully fast."

I let out a helpless groan. "Sure, I liked him. Maybe I even liked him too much." I threw up my hands. "I mean, every female on the face of the planet is in love with him—which is exactly my point. With someone like Brandon Fyfe, any kind of relationship is too risky. You said it yourself. I just needed to get him out of my system. I'm happy with my closure."

"Did you ever respond when he was texting you those first few weeks after he left for that on-location shoot?"

I grimaced. "Of course I did. I'm not a monster. I was really polite."

She stifled her chuckle. "Wow, I'll bet you were. 'I politely decline your request for a relationship'."

I rolled my eyes. "It's not like it's a big deal. I heard he started dating his co-star on that new production. Not that I was surprised. It's better this way." I managed not to wince as I relayed the information. If there was ever any more evidence that I should step back and protect myself from getting hurt any further, it was this.

"How do you know that?" Annie raised an eyebrow. "You still follow him on socials?"

It was pointless to lie so I nodded. "And guess what? His new PA is a guy."

Annie nodded in approval. "Oh, clever."

"Of course, now everyone on social media thinks he's gay."

"Typical." She shook her head in mirth. "Well, you know what they say. Haters gonna hate."

"So true."

"I thought I heard he was going to announce something about his career. Do you think maybe he's planning to take a break from the show and pursue other things?"

"Maybe." I shrugged. "Maybe he's finally managed to negotiate his way out of his current contract. Who knows? Either way, whatever he's got going on in the future, I just...wish him well."

Annie shot me a look. "But...you're still waiting for him."

"No, I'm not."

"Right." She narrowed her eyes at me. "That's why you haven't let me set you up on any dates these past few months."

"That's different. Besides, I don't know if I still trust your taste in men," I teased. "I mean, the ones you won't want to keep for yourself."

She gave me a playful shove. "Mean!"

"Look," I started with a resigned sigh. "I'm sure the right guy will come at the right time. Maybe this time, someone actually attainable. Someone sweet. Someone *not* my client or my boss who I'm actually forbidden to go out with, you know? It could happen."

Annie shook her head as she mused, "Man, say what you want. That is so Hollywood."

***

Swiping my ID badge on the scanner, I pushed open the glass door to the office. "Morning, Eileen." I waved at the lady at reception before heading for my desk to drop off my bag.

The two-storey building was dated and musty, certainly not as big as the *Lightscape* lot, but being one of the smaller studios in Hollywood, an up-and-coming independent, who occasionally contracted to the big companies, it was an ideal place for building my portfolio.

I was now part of a ten-person team to write twenty episodes of an office sitcom's first season.

It seemed Nancy Myers had notable feedback regarding my screenplay, and with her recommendation (and Debra's), the company directors had decided to incorporate some of my work into their new production.

It was definitely the biggest thing that had ever happened to me.

For the last few months, I'd worked with the rest of the writers to develop and polish the show. It made for many, many sleepless nights when all I could think about was creating fresh twists to old tropes, thinking through plot holes, breaking down character arcs, and using my very vivid imagination to construct scenarios.

I supposed one could say I was now eating, sleeping, and breathing the work. Somehow, I'd found exactly what I wanted to do, something I could be truly passionate about.

Within myself. For myself.

Not just for someone else.

Still a bit overwhelmed some days, but definitely grateful.

Yes, grateful to Brandon Fyfe too.

He'd believed in me. The only reason Nancy had even picked up my script in the first place was because of him—who, with his own raft of professional experience, seemed also to have a knack for spotting raw talent.

I would always be grateful to him for giving me direction.

And I liked to think that even if we didn't end up together, Brandon Fyfe had been a huge influence in my life. And that way, it was a comfort to think that some part of him would always be with me.

Bella, one of the other assistant writers on the show, swung by my desk to beckon me over. "We're starting in ten minutes, Rye. Let's go."

I gave her a nod. "Right." Organizing some folders in my hand, I followed her down the hall to the other side of the building with the larger meeting rooms.

I nearly had to wade through the large crowd in the hallway. But since this was my first time attending auditions, I didn't figure there was anything unusual about it.

Slipping into the room behind Bella, I took my seat beside her in the corner, while the casting director, the head writer, and the producer sat at the big table up front.

I pulled out my phone to get ready to take notes. I was still rifling through the pages of the audition scene when the door creaked open wider again to let the first actor in.

"Hi. I'm Brandon Fyfe—"

My head snapped up in alert, and even from the back of the room, I easily met his already dancing blue eyes.

Wearing his usual leather jacket, that wavy, tousled hair falling partway across his forehead, I could have sworn he looked even hotter than I'd ever seen him before.

A shadow of a smirk hung around his mouth as he went on, "Here to read for 'Jack.'"

A thrill shot up my spine, my heart pounding in my ears as warmth flooded every part of me.

I couldn't help but smile back—because the first thing I thought of was that Brandon was finally auditioning for a sitcom. He was finally going to get what he really wanted. He was reaching for his dream too.

Even if I had literally nothing to do with him anymore, I was still so proud and happy for him. It looked like we'd both ended up exactly where we wanted to be.

The rest of the auditions went by in a blur.

I tried not to think of any other implications to Brandon's presence.

I wanted to assume that my new co-workers knew nothing about what had happened between us. Certainly, nobody had ever breathed a word about Brandon Fyfe to me since I was hired here.

I didn't want to start another wildfire of rumors, but I couldn't help myself. By the time we could take a break and everyone filed out of the room, I sprinted out the door, down the stairs, and out of the building.

I didn't want to stop to think either. I just knew I wanted to see him again.

I was ready to see him again.

I was ready to sprint to the bus stop to head out to the Lightscape studios. Maybe drop by his apartment. I was already reaching for my phone so I could call ahead to figure out where he was, but I screeched to a stop in the lobby.

Brandon was still here. He was by the doors, speaking to one of the studio directors. Shaking his hand, saying how enthusiastic he was about the new show and how he was hoping for a favorable result.

Meanwhile, several of my colleagues were wandering past semi-casually, their mouths hanging open, or in frenzied whispers among themselves, completely star-struck. Of course, I absolutely couldn't blame them.

As soon as the director walked away, Brandon's gaze turned to me. Not even seeming surprised at all, his smile widened as those deep blue eyes met mine.

Another wonderful shiver ran up my spine.

Maybe it had been six months, but right then, it felt like no time at all had passed between us.

As I crossed the lobby toward him, he stuck his hands in his pockets. He lifted those broad shoulders in question. "What are my chances of being cast, do you think? It is a significant detour from my usual roles." His nose was wrinkled as if he was uncertain. As if Mr. Arrogant Ego could be any uncertain about being offered *any* role he ever wanted.

I couldn't help a mocking glare before meeting his gaze evenly. "Well, I happen to have it on good authority that the role was written for you."

Brandon pursed his lips, giving me a suggestive look as he took a step closer. "That's interesting. So...does that mean it won't be considered an unfair advantage if I sleep with an assistant writer on the show?"

My smile widening, my shoulders shook with mirth. A teensy bit wary, I glanced around the small-ish crowd of on-lookers milling about. "Oh, Brandon Fyfe, you are so going to get me into so much trouble again."

He cracked a self-satisfied grin. "How about dinner first? And then trouble." A hint of mischief laced his features. "Maybe tomorrow night? If you'll recall, that's—"

"Tomorrow night, that's—" I'd started to say before we both finished.

"Cheat day."

His gaze soft, Brandon touched my cheek. "You remember."

Looking into those intense eyes again, I didn't have to ask if he still liked me. I didn't even have to ask if he was still going out with that actress. And I definitely didn't care anymore who was watching us.

Absolutely nothing else mattered.

When he leaned over to press his lips against mine, I knew.

This was the time. This was the place.

Everything was perfect.

27

Epilogue

Much later

"Is it time to go?" Brandon strolled back into his bedroom, already dressed in a burgundy sweater that complimented those shoulders and designer pants that complimented...other things. "We're supposed to meet Ian and Zoe in half an hour and it's way across town."

Standing in front of the mirror, I put on my earrings. "Any idea what this big announcement is that they're saying they want to tell us?"

He shook his head. "I have no idea. I mean, just last week, they were at each other's throats. I really almost thought one of them was going to choke the other."

I had to chuckle at the thought that popped into my mind. "Sounds like how I felt about you when we first met."

Brandon gave me a narrow-eyed, feigned offended look, but his only response was coming over to wrap his arms around me. "Didn't you say you fell for me at first sight?"

"Um, I'm pretty sure *you* said that about me," I countered with a devious smirk.

He dug his nose in my neck in that totally Brandon Fyfe way. "I missed you the other night," he murmured, nuzzling beneath my ear. "I thought you were busy when you were my PA, but it seems being a writer is worse."

"You're the one who's busy," I pointed out with a sideways glance up to him. "I don't think those lead role offers have stopped coming yet. Is Debra worried at all about confusing your brand now that you're being offered all these kinds of versatile roles?"

"Well, remember she and I have this new thing where I get more freedom to choose the projects I take on now. I think as long as I keep booking them by the truckloads, she'll be happy."

"I'll bet. I already can't turn around in the city without seeing some giant billboard with your huge face on it."

"Good," Brandon huffed, self-satisfied. "I don't want you to ever stop thinking about me."

I had to laugh. "I already think about you at work all day. 'Jack' is turning out to be a very compelling character to write for our show. Our head writer even said that he's a perfectly nuanced character. He said that. In front of everyone. I couldn't even believe it!" My cheeks warmed from pride and pleasure.

"Well, that's because he was your idea," Brandon pointed out. "I'm so happy for you."

I turned around so I could look into those intensely gorgeous eyes. "Not as happy as I am for you."

"I'm happy for us," he concluded, giving me a squeezing hug. Dropping his arms after a moment, he cleared his throat. "Are you sure we're not late yet?"

Pulling away to finish getting ready, I shot him a curious look. "Why are you so concerned about being late for a change? It's usually always me that's trying to get you to hurry up."

"Hey." He gestured to his face. "It's not easy to look as hot as this all the time, you know?"

I stifled my laugh. My gaze darted around, checking surfaces. There was no clock in the room for me to check the time. "Where's my watch?"

"Your what?"

I tapped my empty wrist as I walked around. "My watch. I'm pretty sure it's in here somewhere."

Brandon gave a shrug. "It's probably in the same drawer where you leave things." His tone turned chiding, "I'll say it again—why don't you just leave some of your stuff here to make it easier for you?"

"I have *some* stuff here. I'm already here most nights," I reminded him.

Brandon hadn't actually asked outright, though our conversations lately had been starting to circle around the same topic. I thought it was still a bit too soon to move in together, but even Annie had been nagging me to lock this down. As if there was no chance of me getting it better elsewhere.

Of course, I was a hundred percent sure she wasn't wrong.

It hadn't entirely been a picnic getting a handle on dating Hollywood's hottest actor. For starters, the paparazzi were always everywhere. Also, I got a lot of hate on Brandon's social media accounts—since *obviously* I didn't deserve him, everyone thought I was too plain-looking, and also, why wasn't I a tall, blonde two-time Emmy award winner, perfect actress with a PhD and a clothing line, right?

But all Brandon needed to do was look at me with those deep blue eyes filled with all the love in the world and I would easily run out of cares to give.

I was proud of myself. I was proud of where I was in my career and what I'd achieved so far. I felt I'd barely only scratched the surface of the amazing potential opportunities with my job and I was truly hopeful for the future.

Walking around to my usual bedside table, I pulled open the drawer and a small, square box slid forward with a thump. The kind of distinctively small, square box that anyone who had ever watched a romance movie would know exactly what it was for.

I blinked, stopping short. "What the..." I mumbled before glancing up to meet Brandon's already mischievously self-assured gaze. "Is that a watch box?"

He stuck his hands in his pockets as he walked over. "It's a box. But I imagine you have to open it to find out what's inside."

My jaw nearly dropped. "Brandon," I warned. "That's not a ring, is it? It's a watch, right? You put my watch in a fancy box?"

Running his hands through his hair, he chuckled as if in disbelief. "There's really no surprising you, is there?" He leaned over to kiss my cheek, whispering, "It's a ring."

Before I could gasp in shock, he went on.

"But—" Brandon turned me toward him to peer at my face, a concerned crease on his forehead. "You don't have to open it unless you're ready."

Sucking in an appreciative albeit elated breath, my heart swelled. Typical Brandon and all his perfect plans. I felt so full I thought I might burst. I wished there were better words to say everything I meant right at that moment. But I bet even the best writers in the world could only defer to the same one all-encompassing sentiment.

I gazed up at his face, almost with a helpless shrug. "I love you."

That charming smile on his gorgeous face broadened so wide, I almost swooned all over again, even as he murmured his husky response, "Right back at ya."

***

The End.

Sneak Peek: When They Do

Alex Keaton is the hottest playboy on the West Coast, living the carefree single life. That is until his best friend decides to get married. And he finds himself chasing after the absolute last girl he would have ever imagined.

***

I was getting some drink refills for me and my date (which was code for flirting with the hot female bartender) when Janice found me at the bar.

"Hey," I greeted over the noise of the party. "Tyler here yet?"

Janice yelled in my ear. "He's on his way," she said. "He's picking up Claire from some law school alumni event. Where's Candace?"

"Charmaine," I corrected.

"Oh, so you do bother to know their names?" Janice mused.

I had to laugh. "Why do you always underestimate me?" I asked her. "I can be a perfectly decent gentleman when I want to be."

She wiggled her eyebrows in agreement. "Yeah," she said wryly. "I can see that from your unnecessary tipping at an open bar—oh, finally!" she exclaimed, starting to wave both hands as if to get someone's attention from across the way. "Ty!" she called out.

And when I glanced over, I had to blink myself out of a startle. Tyler was making his way up to the pool area where we were. But my eyes had snapped straight to Claire who was right behind him.

She looked jaw-dropping hot!

She was wearing a low-cut snug little white number and her light brown hair was down her shoulders, wavy and tousled.

"Damn girl, you lookin' fine tonight," Janice commented, giving Claire an appraising look as she and Tyler approached us.

Claire gave her a deadpan look before stealing her drink. "Is that alcohol? Great." And she chugged it down quickly.

Janice's forehead creased. "Something wrong, sweetie?"

"No, no, just busy," Claire dismissed quickly. "Some of the senior partners just decided to throw this case referral down the ranks, and between that and dealing with the interns—"

I wasn't listening to the conversation but I was still staring at Claire. I would never have imagined that that body had been hiding under her usual three-piece business casual attire. Tyler had to elbow me to snap out of it.

He shot me a strange look. "Bro, you checkin' out Claire?"

"What? No," I replied quickly, instinctively, before I stopped short. "I mean, yes. Hell yes," I amended, figuring there was no shame in admitting it.

"She does look different tonight, doesn't she?" Tyler commented.

"Different," I echoed. That was an understatement.

"Have you seen Marco yet?" he asked me.

"Oh, uh." I blinked a few times to clear my head. "Not yet actually." I panned my gaze around the crowd and spotted Nina quickly. She was wearing a shiny silver dress so it was easy to spot her. "There's Nina though. I bet if you stand close to her long enough, Marco will turn up," I remarked with a bit of sarcasm.

"Come on, Jan." Tyler took Janice's hand to pull her along in pursuit of Marco and/or Nina, leaving Claire standing beside me.

She didn't say anything. She wasn't even looking at me. But she took one of the glasses I was holding and drained it quickly. I had to grin. "I see time away from Marco is agreeing with you," I commented, giving her look another once-over.

"Oh my god." Claire shot me an annoyed look. "Would you just shut up? I don't want to talk about it."

"Jeez, someone's having a really bad day," I noted passively, then offered the other glass of wine I had to her. "My offer still stands, you know," I said with another grin. "Whenever you want to get that palette cleansed."

Naturally, I had seen Claire's look of scorn before but it was particularly prickly tonight. "It's that fast, is it?" she cut in, before declaring. "Just because Marco's got a new girlfriend doesn't mean you're suddenly allowed to hit on me."

Just then, I noticed Claire's gaze distract somewhere and I looked up to see what it was.

Tyler and Janice had found Marco and Nina. Marco, inexplicably, was also wearing a shiny silver shirt for tonight's party.

I was about to snicker and remark something insulting about matching couple outfits to Claire, but before I could say anything, Claire grabbed my second glass of wine, chugged it down quickly, then whirled around to walk away.

I tried to see where she went but she was quickly swallowed up by the party crowd.

* * *

Enjoyed the preview? **When They Do** is also available to purchase at your favorite bookstore.

Sneak Peek: Crushing on You

He was her biggest high school crush. Now, he's the subject of her Ph.D. Goal: Don't get distracted.

***

As she crossed Holly Grove, the repeated pounding of a rubber ball echoing against the court floor and the energetic squeaking of shoes indicated that she was headed to the right place.

Looking up, her quick scan of the ten or so bodies playing basketball found 'the man' himself—tall, blond Connell Matthews, just as he intercepted the ball for a rebound.

He took a step back into a lay out to launch the ball into a perfect arc straight swish into the basket.

Like it was choreographed.

Like it was some kind of scene from a movie and he was the star.

Except interestingly, after years of conscious training, Ingrid's stomach no longer burst with butterflies at the mere sight of him, and for a real moment, she was relieved.

The way Felicia had been building it up had frayed Ingrid's nerves, making her doubt she would even be able to do this, making her doubt her conviction.

But Ingrid had been right. It had been so long ago. She was no longer the mousy nerd in high school that fluttered every time he smiled, and craned her neck whenever he walked past. College had pulled (more like forced) her out of her shell, and her acceptance into one of the top grad schools in the country had given her enough confidence that she wasn't just some dumb nobody.

She could totally do this.

It was just work.

With that assurance and a nod to herself, Ingrid set up her laptop on one of the stone benches at the picnic area lining the basketball court. She figured she would just wait for a water break, approach the man-of-the-hour, give him the calling card with the QR code so he could respond to her survey over the internet, and she'd be back home before dinner.

Easy peasy.

A few other sweaty guys were hanging around the benches across the basketball court, gulping down bottles of water, roughhousing among themselves as they waited for their next turn to play. A couple of groups of younger girls were also watching the game themselves and it didn't take a Ph.D. to figure out why.

Sure, one or two more hot guys were playing ball right then too but it was no doubt mainly Connell Matthews who was drawing in the crowd.

Ingrid had seen him play basketball so often in the past, she knew exactly what she would see if she looked up to watch. He would dominate the court like he owned it. He was very determined, very creative, always graceful, and always mesmerizing.

Irrelevant things she already knew, so she simply focused on her work.

She bent her head to re-read a few responses she had already recorded while the game continued, and after a few minutes, she'd drowned out the whoops and yelling coming from the game as she took down a few preparatory notes.

That was if Connell Matthews might be part of the study now, she had to adjust a few assumptions and parameters so that—

"WATCH OUT!"

By the time Ingrid looked up, it was too late.

The spinning orange ball came hurtling at her face.

"Aahh—!" Ingrid toppled back off the bench, her laptop clattering to the concrete floor. Her vision blurred and the world spun a little bit as she landed on her back with a thump.

There were some shouts, some hasty steps thudding on the pavement.

Before she knew it, strong arms were braced around her back to prop her upright.

"Oh, shoot—I'm so sorry. Are you okay?"

Ingrid barely registered the deep, rich voice that was tinged with genuine concern. She blinked hard, trying to get her ears to stop ringing. The sore spot on her forehead where the ball hit her was most likely red, except since she was also flushed from embarrassment, people probably couldn't tell.

Was she okay? Seriously?

Mortification flushed right through her. So did a rush of about a dozen flashbacks of utterly embarrassing past incidents involving Connell Matthews. Why did she always have to be embarrassed around him?

This was one of the reasons she had been adamant to get over her senseless crush—to avoid getting into any more of these situations, and for a moment, she was incensed. This was all Felicia's fault!

Ingrid should have known better than to listen to Felicia and let herself get manipulated in the first place. And now look what's happened!

Ingrid squeezed her eyes shut to get her bearings back as she stifled a groan in ridicule. "Is that a rhetorical question or a shocking indictment of whatever educational institution you're a product of?"

At her dry retort, a slightly bemused chuckle seemed to catch in his throat. "What?"

When Ingrid opened her eyes to meet his gaze, his forehead was wrinkled with worry, eyebrows furrowed as he looked her over.

It was curious. Naturally, she had seen so many pictures of Connell Matthews in the past but seeing those eyes, in person, mere inches away, Ingrid still froze at the gorgeous blue of their color, causing a flustered stir in her stomach.

Connell's hair was matted to his forehead and his neck from sweat but Ingrid had most definitely never been quite this close to him to appreciate the chiseled cut of his jaw and those high cheekbones.

His muscle-T basketball hoodie hid nothing of his broad shoulders, that strong chest, and those toned arms. As an athlete, he had always been fit but in the last seven years, hot-as-hell high school jock Connell Matthews had certainly grown up.

His arm was still around her back to help her sit up and somehow, a faint scent of his cologne had survived the basketball game. At his proximity, sixteen-year-old Ingrid's heart skipped a beat.

Oh, crap.

***

Enjoyed the preview? **Crushing on You** is available to purchase at your favorite bookstore.

About the Author

SARA BELLCAMP lives in New Zealand with her husband and two kids. She mainly writes offbeat, quirky sweet contemporary romance under the pen name **Sara Breaker**. Simple, sweet stories and epic happy endings.

Suburban mum by day and author by night, she loves to live vicariously through her characters. They don't have to vacuum all day long and are always guaranteed happy endings, no matter how melodramatic she writes them.

She likes binge-watching TV shows and reading books that take you through the requisite ups and downs of a good story, breaks your heart, puts it back together, bam! happy ending—but then still have enough time to wash the dishes after.

Subscribe to her mailing list and get a FREE e-book!

https://subscribe.breakerworlds.com/romance